WALSH'S LAIR BOOK 5

KATHI S. BARTON

This is a work of fiction. Names, characters, places, and incidents are products of the author's imagination or are used fictitiously and are not to be construed as real. Any resemblance to actual events, locations, organizations, or persons, living or dead, is entirely coincidental.

World Castle Publishing, LLC
Pensacola, Florida
Copyright © 2025 Kathi S. Barton
Hardback ISBN: 9798271609107
Paperback ISBN: 9798891264847
eBook ISBN: 9798891264854
First Edition World Castle Publishing, LLC, November 3, 2025
http://www.worldcastlepublishing.com
Licensing Notes
Cover: Cover Designs by Karen
Editor: Karen Fuller

Prologue

The Gathering Storm
~~The Peace of being without war~~
~~Evenness of mind, temper, and composure~~
~~ Created by imagination, invention, and design~~

Storm walked around the little store listening to the gossip about one of the biggest disasters ever recorded — at least how these people were now witnessing it. She shook her head in amazement. How could humans be so insensitive? Not to mention stupid. That was one of the million and one reasons that she didn't hang out with humans for too long. They were not only for the most part clueless, but they seemed to have rose colored glasses on all the time. The rumor mill was running full blast, it seemed today.

"They say that thousands of those bastards are dead. The whole place just split the roads and ate'em right up. Can't you just imagine what they were thinking when they were being swallowed up like that? I can't, I tell you what." The man behind the counter had himself a great audience, and he was taking full advantage of it today.

"Heard tell that them there houses just toppled

over like the kids' blocks. Smashing people while they slept in their beds." The man speaking shook his head. "Mercy sakes alive, it sure did a nasty bit of business over there on that street."

"God is taking some sort of vengeance on them there foreigners. Sure as I'm a 'sitting here, it's God doing them people in." She actually had to physically close her own mouth when the person made that statement. "They should have stayed in their own place, not here where we people are." Storm wondered if a one of the people standing at the counter knew that they were all foreigners to this land.

She also wondered what they'd say about her and her sister if they knew what they really were, which made her smile. She wasn't going to speculate on it too much, but they'd have plenty to say, there was no doubt about that. They couldn't have gotten more foreigners than they were.

Storm and her twin sister, Ember, were time adjusters for the world. They, like a great many other beings, moved throughout time and made slight adjustments in the fabric of reality when and where it was needed, smoothing out the lines so that it looked untouched, perfect. They'd been doing it longer than any of the beings in this room had been alive. And they would continue to do so long after they were nothing more than dust in their graves. Humans and shifters alike had no idea how many times they'd been rescued from their own stupidity.

To do their jobs, they would travel back and forth, sliding into whatever persona was needed to blend into the world they were in. It took great strength and lots of practice to even attempt what they did for the world. Sometimes they were the only ones standing between the extinction of mankind and the world being overpopulated at any given time. Storm caught a reflection of her face as she walked around the little odds and ends store.

Tall, at just over six-foot, Storm was well-proportioned and athletic. Of course, no one would see that under her long dress and equally long sleeves. Her long dark hair, when not pulled into a tight bun at the back of her head as it was now, hung nearly to her waist in springy corkscrew ringlets. Her wings, too, pressed tightly against her back and legs, only giving a small hint to what she really was.

Her skin, like her sisters was alabaster and smooth as velvet. The only mark that marred their skin was the tattoo of their kind. It was a dragon that wore the wings that curled around their back, clawed hands seemingly holding onto their shoulders, while the tail trailed down their ribs and wrapped around their legs. Storms on her left leg, Embers to her right.

When their wings were spread and covering

their arms from shoulders to their wrists, it would be, she supposed, frightening to anyone who would see her without any knowledge of what she was. Smiling at the men when they tipped their hats at her, she put her purchases on the counter and waited for her turn to be waited on.

At the moment Storm was in the year nineteen hundred and twenty-three in the body of a school teacher about to start "schooling" the area children in their reading, writing, and arithmetic. It was the closest body that fit her size when she popped into the time zone. The teacher would have no memories of her being Storm for a bit. There would be a slight accident, a small tumble that would alter her memories. Not that she'd remember Storm and what she had done, but the teacher would recover easily and never be the wiser of what she'd done for her world.

This time, working in this area, it had been a small fix. A mountain had come down on a family that was digging for clay and killed the youngest child. Storm had been tasked to save the child; her future and that of a great many generations beyond her hadn't been born if she'd been killed. Saving the family, simply making them later than they had planned to the mountainside had done the trick. The mom, always so organized, would forget to bring the cold water she'd stored in the creek that ran by their home to keep it nice and chilled for them all. Storm loved it when it was something like this had been.

There were times when whole realities had to be altered. Generations needed to be moved ahead to save someone. Sometimes it was to save a being or one of the descendants of a human who was needed in the future. Other times it was to erase a horrific time in the lives of humans — mostly it was natural disasters where many deaths occurred. Humans, for the most part, would change up their entire lives, nothing to do with the ones that had been killed, because they were witnesses to something so horrific that they had seen. It was all in the timing, she knew.

Other times, it was the consequences of the disaster that were too large and affected too many things when they rippled down through the ages and had to be removed. Something as simple as a house being crushed with their things inside. It could have been the witnessing of a family pet being killed. Any and all things that would alter everything, and it was up to them to repair the damage that had been done.

As Time Displacement Officers, they were there to ensure that the shifts were smooth, with no overlapping lines after the time frame was removed or fixed. Storm would watch an event, something that she'd fixed a thousand times to make sure that things were normal. However, gifted humans or small children saw the flaws. It was easily explained as déjà vu. Or a dream too. Small children would complain to their mothers or fathers about how they'd done this before, only to be told that they were wrong. Poor little tykes. She would believe her children, should she ever find herself a mate. Not that she was looking for one.

Storm was also there to capture another of their kind and bring him to justice. It was he who had moved the family to the mountain for the one to be killed. And he would have profited from the disaster had she not been there when it unfolded. Neither was something that they could let happen. Everything you did, even from pulling a leaf off a tree, would affect generations of families, she'd come to learn. And that was the very thing that the other being was doing — affecting generations of families for his own profit.

His name was Grail. He had been altering reality to suit his own personal gain and to profit for a while now, but no one could catch him. She was determined to find and make him pay before he could cause any more trouble. Altering a timeline too often would lead to sloppy work, time twitches that people would notice. And that was something that she was afraid of more than anything that she'd encountered in the human world. Too many glitches would wake the residents of the world to question what was going on, and it would — nearly all the time, make them question their sanity.

Profit and notoriety from their jobs, both of which were laws that carried the sentence of death if broken, were what he had been doing today. Storm shuddered at the thought of the death he would endure when they took him back to Chilast, their magical realm. Death would not come easily or quickly for one like Grail. He had to know that. So why was he doing this when he knew it was only a matter of time before he was caught? No one knew the answer to that.

They didn't have the people to chase after him and keep the world and its people safe. As it was now, they were stretched to the limit. Working from sunup to sundown and all in between, too, it had been so long since she'd had a day off that she wanted to just lie down, pull some leaves over her, and get to sleep for about a thousand years.

Storm's twin sister, Ember, had gone to Tokyo to study and gather names of their kind for the continuation of their race. So far, all she'd been able to find was the list of the dead. All of the dragons that had come after her and a few others that had been killed were on that list. That wasn't doing any of them a bit of good, and they all knew it. They were aging out, the lot of them, and there wasn't anything that they could do about it.

It didn't bother their kind when they would

wind time backward. It was the moving of time forward that would harm them. Time, it would add, even if it was only a click of a second to their age. And having to look at something over and over, forward and back, it might well add as many as ten minutes onto their long lives. After a while and all those adding up, a dragon would age quicker, worn down by time and effort, because without rest and some time off, they'd just fade away like all the other creatures in the world.

Storm had been sent to the Americas for her assignment to find and collect Grail before he could act on his plan. If they didn't find him, and soon, all the work they'd kept up with would be useless. They'd all be dead, and there wasn't anything that could be done about it after that.

But she had a feeling this time was different. They knew his plan, what he had needed, and who to make himself in a new body to get away. It was what they had needed, what they were counting on to bring him to heel and to make all their lives safer without him in their worlds.

There was supposed to be a natural disaster, a large-scale shift in the earth's interior makeup that would cause the entire state of California to drift into the deep ocean and sink, killing all the inhabitants there. There were people there that he needed to complete the next phase of his power play against his own kind. She had been sent there to make sure that it didn't happen and to bring Grail to the Laws of the Realm.

Those people, men and women alike, were the pioneers of the future that Grail was manipulating. Their collective knowledge would be passed down to their children and then on to the next generation. They were brilliant and would revolutionize the world with Grail's backing and help. And not in a good way that would only benefit themselves and no one else.

They, like Grail, were evil and only thought to gain untold riches and wealth from sources within the different time lines that he was supposed to care for. From future records, the Time Displacement Office – the TDO and the Elders of their kind, knew that he had taken this opportunity to steal them away, along with all their equipment. In the aftermath of the devastating slide, everyone would assume they had been killed as well. After decades of exhaustive tracing and retracing the lines of time back, the TDO knew this was where he made his first move to bring his plan to fruition.

But the quake, the distraction, as if it were never to happen. At least not where it had happened in the history they had studied. It had happened the day before in Tokyo, where Ember was studying and gathering information. She worried for her, and when she couldn't contact her, she just knew the worst had happened.

Storm had been trying to contact her sister for hours without luck. They were both immortals and could shift and fly away if danger was imminent, but with the suddenness of the quake in Tokyo and the horrific scale on which it had occurred, Storm feared her sister needed her and needed her now.

Storm felt the first touches of Ember as she exited the store. The feelings got stronger the more Storm concentrated on her sister's touch to her mind. It was all she could do to keep an eye out as to where she was going, and thinking about her sister at the same time.

"Are you all right? I've been trying to reach you for hours. What's happened?" Storm said as soon as the link was snapped into place between them. Ember told her that she was fine, never better. "I've been so worried about you that I can barely breathe."

"There are signs of him here. I have contacted several of our kind in the area, and they say that he stayed with them for one night, two days ago. I can smell him and his poison here deep within the belly of the mountains where the records are kept." Storm smiled at her greeting. Ember was never one to mince words when it came to their jobs.

"Did he hurt any of them? Ask them for their help?" It would be just like him to murder them all just to throw them off his scent. But, at least for now, he only killed when he could gain from it.

"No. He spoke to no one but the people who were kind enough to allow him to rest at their dwellings. They say that he had a satchel with him, but he didn't seem to want to let anyone know what was in it. The Elders found a small thread, or we may not have known that he was even here. He's either getting better at hiding from us or we're getting worse at our job, Storm."

"It's the same story here. He spent a night with the others here and then left. No one mentioned a satchel, though. He moved the place, altered the fabric where he had been. Ember, he didn't take the people he had before. Somehow, he has modified the events of that night yet again." Storm was suddenly terrified, and she was sure things were going to get worse before they caught up with him. "What do you suppose was in the sachet? I mean, is it important you think?"

"Moran, the one who was closest to him when he was here, said that it had photos in it. Some of them were old tin types, others digital, and one was a hologram. He thought they looked like me, but the eyes were the wrong color. I'm assuming that it must have been of you. Also, from what I could gather, there were images of the people in California. There…there was a picture of a man, as well. One that we've not encountered in all our searches as yet."

"Photos? Maybe he's using outside help to try to find these people. Makes sense that he would have pictures. He'd have to show them who to look for, right? No, he didn't take anyone as far as I can tell. It's...he's changed everything again."

There was a long pause through their connection; Storm could feel her sister's tension.

"What is it? Something has happened. Tell me."

"The Elders they called to me two days ago. They needed an extraction. I...they had me take a human away from a deadly shooting. I've no details yet, but he is to be guarded at all costs. I have him deep within the mountains with us. He is curious but not frightened. I think that is why there was a shift in the location of where the quake happened. I think we missed this man somehow, and we angered Grail by taking him. He was in one of the photos in Grail's collection. Storm, this man, he was to die."

"Who is he? Had he been taken by Grail before? Is he one of Grail's minions?" She was more worried for her sister's safety than ever before.

"No. He isn't like that. His mind and body are pure. His spirit is clear. The shooting I took him from killed the others like him – men who uphold the law. I barely made it to him before the killings began in a house in New York. My wings were damaged slightly;

I've been in a healing sleep until now." Still, Storm could feel her hesitation.

"Tell me the rest, Ember." She could have looked, she supposed, but in her current state, she knew that she'd hurt her sister. And she didn't want to do that. Hurting her would hurt her as well. "Ember?"

"I've been…the others here, we've…I've formed a bond with one. I've found my mate, Storm. After all this time, I've found my mate, and I'm afraid. Not of him, no, but what this is going to mean for the two of us. They will curtail my work soon."

Storm felt her heart stutter to a stop. Her mate, Ember, had found her mate. Storm moved to the outer wall of the store and leaned heavily against it. This would change everything. Ember could no longer help her with their job. As soon as Storm thought it, she felt horrible. Ember had found her mate; she should be rejoicing.

"Storm, please don't be mad. I didn't mean for this to happen." She had hurt her anyway. The tone of Ember's voice told her that.

"Don't be ridiculous. I'm happy for you. It's just a surprise, that's all. I wish you nothing but happiness and good fortune. I love you." Storm, stronger now because she had heard from Ember and knew that her sister was going to be all right, continued. "I'm going to contact the Elders and see what they want me to do now. You'll be all right for now? You're making sure that you're all safe while you work?"

"Yes, I am fine. Thank you, Sister. I will be waiting for you in our cave. You let me know when you will be arriving, and I'll be watching the sky for you."

Storm hoped it would be that easy, but knowing the Elders as she did, she doubted it very much. They would want something from her, and she'd do it because Storm was loyal to a fault.

~~Devotion to the continued existence of life~~

~~Devotion to the supreme good~~

~~Pure condition of body and mind~~

It was against the Laws of the Realm to appear before the Elders in any other form than the one in which you had been born to. She didn't mind that so much as she loved being a dragon whenever she could. As soon as Storm arrived at the castle, she reached out to touch the magistrate to set up a meeting with the Elders and the Queen. She was both surprised and terrified that they had readily agreed to see her as soon as she had eaten and shifted.

Food was brought to her, and she enjoyed a large meal. As soon as she had finished, she knew that she needed to complete her mission and get back to her sister. Moving to the outdoor paddock just outside her suite of rooms, Storm began her shift.

She loved to be a human. Storm loved the soft textures of their skin, the feel of the hair upon the body. She also loved the way the fingers bent and was able to grasp things within them. The light feelings of simply walking would make her giddy with anticipation of stepping into the grass or sand with her bare feet. But to be her true self, there was nothing better.

Storm was a dragon, an Enneahedral Dragon — also known as a Ninefold Dragon. She was as rare as any being could be. Storm was the ninth daughter of nine daughters for nine generations. When she had been hatched, she had inherited all the elementals of the earth and the nine directives as well. Her powers were nine times that of her sister Ember — even though she'd only been seconds behind her in coming out of her shell and abilities that went beyond any other dragons.

With being the ninth in so many lines, Storm was to be Queen of their kind as soon as she found a mate worthy of her and her love. But she was in no hurry to find either. She was too busy to care for a lover and didn't want one slowing her down either.

As soon as she stepped into the magical arena, she let her body respond to the pull of her Dragon. First, her body elongated, her spine curving and pulling, stretching to accommodate the large bulk of her form. Then her feet, dainty and small as a human, they too stretched, and great claws formed at the toes. The wings at her back began pulling away from her body and forming into a great expanse, wide and full. Flapping them once, she felt the blood surge through them, and then she pulled them tight against her body. Her face molded and formed into a massive head, teeth a foot in length and sharp as the talons at her feet filled her mouth, full and lethal. The human skin along her arms became scales of great strength, able to protect her from any weapon, small or large. Her scales shimmered in the moonlight, catching and reflecting the gold and silver that blazed within each protective shell. By the time the shift was complete, Storm was a massive twenty-five feet tall, seventy feet wide with her wingspan, and weighed several tons of pure muscle and bone. She moved to the large door that went directly into the throne room and bowed before the other dragons gathered there, careful of every step that she took.

"Mistress Storm, thank you for coming to see us so quickly. We have much to discuss." Storm dipped her head to hide her confusion. They had expected her?

"You must go to China. We need you to bring back the man Alexander Walsh. It is imperative that he survives. He is vital to the future of our race, to all of us."

"Pardon me, Sire, but my sister, Ember, she

is—" Storm started to tell them what she was sure that they already knew, but they cut her off.

"Ember is going to have a hatchling soon. She must stay hidden. If Grail finds her, he will destroy her and the babe. No, it is you who needs to go and bring him back to us. May we count on you to serve us well, Mistress Storm?"

"Of course." Storm bowed before them and took a step back to leave the room. She was stopped by a slight cough from behind her.

"My lords, have you yet told the Mistress what is expected of her?" Storm startled. The being was small, but in no means diminished in her stature. Standing before her was the strongest being anyone had ever known. Her mother, Queen of the Enneahedral Dragon clan, had swept into the room, her strength preceding her. "I will take it upon myself to do that now. You're dismissed." The people in the room disappeared at her command.

"Mother, you look well." Storm never knew how to speak to her mother, Morning. She had always intimidated her. Now was no different. Her beauty was one of the reasons; the other was that her mother wasn't really the affectionate sort of person. But then neither was she.

"You look beautiful, child. I would like for you to shift and meet me in my private chamber. I should like to speak to you about this mission." Nodding once, her mother smiled. "We'll have a luncheon, you and I. And tea. I should like to speak to you about your other adventures, too, if you would allow it."

Immediately, Storm's body started its shift to human form. Within seconds, she was dressed similarly to her mother in a long silk robe with their crest blazing over their hearts. Storm nearly stepped back from her, as Morning was standing very close. Surprisingly, Morning reached out and hugged her close to her.

The tightness of the hug had tears fill her eyes. It had been forever since her mother had hugged her, much less had hugged her first. Wrapping her arms around her mother, she heard her soft sob, and when she pulled away, her mother turned her back to her and started talking. As if nothing had happened.

"This man, Alex, you will bring him back to us safe. It's important." They were seated in the large room that her mother used when she came to the castle's offices. "I know that your sister is there, but she is breeding now, thank the gods, and it's important to all of us that she be able to deliver her hatchling safely." Her mom sat down, so Storm did the same in an equally ornate chair.

It was not a question, but Storm answered her anyway. "Yes. You can trust me to keep him safe."

"It's not his safety that I worry about, it's yours." Morning shifted on her seat, unease evident on her face and posture. "Alex is your mate. It is determined by the Elders that he will father the next line. His bloodline is strong and pure; he will provide you with love and companionship for the rest of your life and on into the next. You and he and the family you breed will be the ones to destroy evil. "

Storm looked sharply at her mother. No. No, this could not be happening. She did not want a mate chosen for her. She stood and began pacing the room.

"You're angry. I don't blame you. I would be —"

"Pardon me, but you don't know me well enough to judge my anger. I will bring this man to you, but no one is choosing my mate." She turned on her mother, not sure that this was a smart move on her part, but she was pissed. "Was Ember's mate chosen for her as well? I'm sure that she'll be thrilled to know that her life has been arranged for her."

"No, her finding her mate was a surprise to us all. But this man, Alex, he's been chosen as your mate since before he was born. And you will not use that tone with me, young lady. I am still your mother." Storm took a deep breath and then sat down when her mother asked her to.

"I miss said what he was to you, Storm. No one chose him for you. It was written in the tomes of the future. You will mate with him and bring children into this world that will be needed. When I said chosen, I meant that it has been written."

She stalked out of the room and into the courtyard again. This time, she shifted as she ran, her body forming and shaping as she went. By the time she had gone a hundred yards, she was launching herself into the sky and soared across the night.

~~Enjoy great happiness~~
~~Maintain a fond hope for all kind~~
~~Uphold the reparation of magical energy requirements~~

Storm shifted to a human as she touched the ground. Her body threw off its form as if it were a heavy coat she no longer needed. She had landed close to the mouth of the cave where the man Alex was waiting.

Storm had contacted Ember when she left the Realm late last night. Telling her the events that had happened at the castle, but she left out the part of "the man" being her mate. She did not plan on taking him as her mate, so she felt no reason to relay the news. Storm had also asked Ember to have the man waiting for her at the mouth of the cave. Storm did not want to take the time to go down and get him. The sooner she took him to the Elders and finished this assignment, the happier she would be.

"You're to come with me. I'm to take you to the

Chilast," she said when she saw who she assumed was Alexander. She put out her hand to have him come with her.

"I don't think so. Not until someone explains to me what is going on. One minute I'm on a domestic violence call, the next I'm being wrapped in wings and brought here. Wings—I've seen some weird shit as a cop, but wings are something I've never encountered before." Alex sat hard onto the stone next to the wall. He looked stubborn and formidable. She was annoyed but impressed, too.

He was a very handsome man and taller than her by a good half a foot. His hair was dark, as dark as Storm's, but where hers was curly, his was straight and hung just past his shoulders. The shirt he had on had been torn, so she had a delicious view of his hard abs and harder chest. It looked smooth, and her fingers itched to touch, not just his chest, but his entire body. Storm decided that she did not like him and would not be his mate, no matter what anyone said about it.

"I don't have time to explain, so get ready to go." She could feel the attraction to him, and she hated him all the more for it.

Before he could say anything else, the earth shook beneath them. Alex fell to the cave floor, and Storm was thrown to the wall, striking her head hard. While she fought the blackness trying to consume her, she threw a protective shell around Alex.

"Well, hello, Storm. You have something that belongs to me. I want him. Now!" Grail moved into the mouth opening of the cave, and Storm felt his power surge against the spell she had wrapped around Alex. It wouldn't work, of course, she was much stronger than him, but it would weaken her more in protecting the human.

Grail had been a gray Dragon in color when Storm had first met him, his color bleeding into his human form, giving his eyes and hair the same rich colors. Now he was black as pitch. His eyes, once a soft, rich pewter color, were now black with his dark magic and evilness. He was tall, as were all their kind, but he was also heavy. His lack of physical activity not keeping him in the shape he should have been. Though his face, dusky in pallor, was gaunt and shallow. She wondered how he could fly, much less take flight.

"You can't have him. I'm to take him back to the realm." She opened her magic and pushed hard back.

Grail raised his hands, and power appeared in the form of a ball of electricity. The longer he held it, the bigger it grew. If he hit the protection, he would destroy it. Storm needed to get them to safety now.

Storm moved in a flash to stand in front of her assignment. She shifted partway, and her wings fluttered out from her back. She flapped them once, and their powerful movement moved air strongly around the forest and knocked Grail to the ground as he stood in his fragile human form. Turning to Alex, she grabbed him up and ran to the lighted opening just beyond Grail. As she passed him, she felt a searing pain in her back but did not slow her pace. By the time she was in the open light, she was a full dragon, Alex tucked tightly in her talons. She soared high in the air just as Grail screamed at her to come back.

As a dragon, she could see all the areas where it would be safe for them to land. Her vision was perfect, and she could see the heat from any humans or animals below them, not wanting to land where anything could find them. Storm knew she was losing blood, but until she landed and got the man to safety, there was little to nothing she could do. She was getting weaker and knew that she would need to land soon or risk falling and crushing the man she was sent to protect.

Opening her mind, she hoped to be able to speak to the man. It was the way of their kind to be able to talk to their mates when there had been no bond at all between them. Unlike most species, she could have spoken to Alex since his birth had she known about him being what he was to her.

"Are you hurt? I should have asked sooner, but I wanted to get you out of harm's way."

"No. I'm fine. Your claws are digging into me,

but I fear that if you lessen your grip, I feel I'll fall to the earth — unless that is your plan? Tell me, Storm, do you plan to play toss the man into the air and see if you can catch him before he plummets to the earth? If so, could we not play today? I have a very busy schedule tomorrow, and if I'm crushed…well, it could put a crimp in things. No, I think a little pinching is preferable to death. I can smell your blood. How hurt are you?" She told him that she was, but she would heal when they landed. "If there is anything I can do to help you, please let me know. I'm pretty handy to have around."

She smiled at his sense of humor. Storm had not expected that. He was being very calm for a man who was being flown well above the clouds by a huge blue dragon.

"I must land soon to sleep and heal. I know of a place where you'll be safe until I can do both. No one will bother you there." She told him with as much reassurance as she could. Weakness was pulling hard at her, and she did not think she could go much longer.

"So you plan to leave me? I hope you don't expect me to sit around quietly waiting for your return. I may not know what is going on or why that other… what was he anyway?"

"He's a dragon like me. And you will stay where I tell you. You are to live at all costs. I don't have time to placate your feelings, human. I can easily say that you were eaten by Grail, as not. Now be quiet." Storm began her descent.

Pain racked her body, and she knew that the landing was going to be hard. Seconds before she hit the earth, she dropped Alex and tumbled over him, careful not to land on him. As much as he irritated her, she did not want to kill him.

Her body shifted as soon as she stopped rolling, shifting to the last shape she had taken, hiding her true identity from anyone who would come upon her injured body. It was there to provide their kind with surreptitiousness.

Storm sat up just long enough to ensure that Alex was all right, her body and mind already pulling her to sleep. The area where she had taken them was hers; it was safe and hidden well from everyone, including any of her kind. She saw Alex stand and stride toward her just as blackness pulled her under.

~*~

Alex leaned over the woman he had carried into the house he had found a mile or so from where she had fallen. The fire he had lit in the deep fireplace reflected off her face, the reds and golds of the flames casting surreal shadows across her flawless cheeks. She was a beauty, just like her sister, Ember.

There was no doubt to him that the two women

were sisters, as they were identical twins and as alike as any he had ever seen. He moved the dark hair away from her face and ran his fingers down her downy cheek. When she stirred slightly, he grinned. She was by far the most stubborn person he had ever met.

"Why do you look at me like that?" She looked up at him, her voice soft in the hushed room.

"I was thinking about how unlike your sister and you are. You are very beautiful, both of you. But you lack her softness and the...genteel nature that she has. You are strong and stubborn. And I've never wanted to kiss anyone more than I do you."

The expression on her face was priceless. He nearly laughed out loud, but caught himself before it burst forth. He was afraid she would hurt him. Alex was not a stupid man; he had seen what she was, and while it was hard to believe, he was not going to dismiss the fact that she had flown them away from trouble.

"Why?" He asked her what she meant. "Why would you want to kiss me? It's not like I'm all that much. I'm, well, at least for the moment, just a woman who has the ability to change into a great dragon. Nothing special about that."

"Why would I want to kiss you, or why do I think you're stubborn?" He touched her again. He could not seem to help himself. "And you are extremely special.

I've only just thought of this, too. You're extremely special to me for some reason. Do you know why?"

She looked at him for long moments, and he suddenly felt her touch his mind again, this time in a searching way, not to speak. Alex was not sure why he did not block her, but he would not try to fight her if she needed reassurances.

"You're a vampire. They didn't tell me that." She sat up on the side of the bed, but he didn't move back. It put them closer than before, and he was happy with that.

"Yes, I'm a vampire. You're a dragon. I didn't know that you even existed until I met Ember. You say 'they'. Who? And who is that man who tried to kill us?"

"The Elders of our kind, they are the ones who sent me to bring you back to them. The other dragon, whose name is Grail. He's also a dragon like me, a time shifter. Did Ember tell you what we do?" He nodded, and she continued. "He was there to kill you and me because we're supposed to be mates. We are to deliver the next line of dragons. Mother told me that our children were meant to destroy him and his reign. I didn't stick around long enough to hear why. Grail has been building his power base for many years and has been moving through time, making adjustments in the fabric of lives to gather monies to fund his cause — to destroy all dragons but himself. I was in the Americas waiting for Grail to make a move to take a group of scientists away before they were to die, but he came here to get you instead. We had been tracking him for some time. The earthquake that happened in China was the result of his having a temper tantrum. Ember said that she had been sent to save you, but she didn't know why until I spoke to her. You see, you were to die in that last call you went on when on patrol. When Grail realized that you had survived, he unleashed his anger on those people."

"I'm sorry for them. I never meant to cause them harm." He was a good cop, and he never pulled his gun unless it was the only thing left for him to do.

Storm stood up and looked at him. The glow from the fire danced in her eyes. When she licked her lips, he watched, mesmerized by the pink tip moistening her lush lips. "Storm…"

Before he could claim her mouth, he felt himself being tossed across the room, Storm landing across his body, protecting him from falling debris. Her hand clamped tightly across his mouth when he started to speak.

"Grail." She said in a way of explanation. Moving quickly, she stood and pulled him close to her.

"I know you're in there, Storm, my dear. Come out and play with me, and bring our tasty friend along with you. We'll char him up and laugh over the silliness of all this fighting. I can offer you so much more than he could ever."

Alex pressed back against the far wall, flipped Storm around so that her back was now where his had been, and he moved hard to her body.

"As a human, is he mortal? Will he die like a regular man?" Alex moved the thoughts through her mind. The words were fast and hard, urgent even.

"No. Yes. It needs to be silver through his heart, though. But his dragon would protect him by wrapping itself around Grail and taking him away. Grail would sense your movement, and as quick as you are, Grail is much faster. You can't...you can't think to beat him, do you? He'll take you, kill you."

"Do you care, Storm? Would you mourn me if he kills me?" Now his voice was a caress, a stroke along her heart and mind.

Without hesitation, without speaking in his mind, she answered. "Yes. Yes, I would."

"You are mine, understand?" He warned her. At her nod, he kissed her quickly and pulled his gun from his ankle holster. Winking at her, he took her hand and moved to the front of what had once been a small house.

"Please, Alex, please don't do this. He'll kill you." She whispered in his mind again.

"He'll try." When he started to step away, she pulled him back into the semi-darkness. "What?"

"You need to feed from me. I'll strengthen you, protect you. Feed from me and my dragon will know you, and it'll keep you safe, keep us both safe."

Alex looked at her and smiled. He felt his fangs drop into place to feed. The need to sip from her nearly staggered him off his feet.

He wanted to savor her, make her his, and knew from her sister that dragon blood, especially Storm's blood, was poison to those who did not ask and were not given permission before drinking. But for those who had been allowed that rare sip, the benefits were amazing. Alex leaned into her throat, nuzzling her skin, tasting her with his mouth and tongue. Licking the area just over the pulse pounding in her neck, he pulled back slightly and stuck his bite deep and quick. Her moan ran along his skin like a caress.

At the first taste of her essence, he immediately felt the power surge into him. The more he drew from her, the stronger he felt his body getting. Alex was an older vampire, so his strength was not paltry, but with her surging through his veins, he felt extraordinary.

Pulling back reluctantly, he sealed the tiny wounds with a flick of his tongue. Moving his mouth along her jaw, he reached her mouth and sealed his over her heat.

"I know that you're in there, Storm. I demand that you come out now and face me. I have plans for us, plans that do not include that vampire mate of yours. Children of our union will bring me more money than I ever imagined."

Alex backed away from her slightly and saw the lust in her eyes. "If you stay right here, I'll take care of him, and we can get back to where we were before he interrupted us."

"I need to keep you safe. I need to stand at your side." He smiled at her possessive tone.

Moving and taking her hand once again, he hid his gun behind him as they walked forward.

"Ah, the future Queen and her stud. You know, I think I'm going to enjoy killing him. Oh yeah, this is going to be…"

He never finished. As he dropped to the ground, Grail stared at the smoking gun in Alex's hand.

Alex and Storm watched as Grail began to shift into several forms quickly before he simply melted into the ground; his blue blood stained the ground beneath him.

There was a lot to be said for the element of surprise.

~*~

"Sammy, there's a phone call for you. It's your sister." She didn't go into panic mode like she normally did when there was a call for her, but made her way to the community phone, just taking her time. "She said to remind you that it's her birthday and that you should be wanting to do something nice for her."

"Nice? I don't suppose she gave you a price range as to what this nice gift is going to cost me, did she?" The cook told her no, she'd not, but like always, it was going to cost a great deal. "You got that right. I'll tell you what it is if you want to formulate a price range while I'm talking to her."

"You gonna tell her no, aren't you?" She just stared at him. "Yeah, I hope so. She sounds really excited, so I'm going to assume that it's a really nice gift you got for her."

"She works, so I don't understand why… it doesn't matter. I'm not going to pay for anything that she's gotten for herself from me." She picked up the phone and had to wait while her sister talked to someone else. Wanting to hang up, she knew that she'd only call back, and she'd not be happy with her. Suddenly, she was talking to her.

"I got me the most amazing gift from you." All she said was no. "Don't be like that. You don't even know what it is."

"I've told you this before, Justine. I'm not going to be buying you gifts for your birthday anymore that I didn't pick out on my own." She said that she doesn't get her what she wants. "I can't afford what you want. And you're nearly forty years old. You're a little old to be hoping for a gift from your little sister."

"Why do you have to be like that? Bringing up my age two days before my birthday." She said that her birthday was in two weeks. "So. I should have a month to celebrate my birthday. It's not every day that someone turns forty, as you might know."

"I don't care. I'm not going to foot the price of whatever you think that I'm going to be paying for." She said that she'd already put down a deposit. "Get it back. I'm not going to be footing the bill for anything. I thought you would have learned your lesson last year and the years before. I'm not going to be paying for whatever you got yourself. That's final."

"You're so mean to me all the time, Sammy. I just don't understand you. I'll get my deposit back, but I'm not going to be happy with you for a year. You can bet you're not going to be getting anything from me either when your birthday comes around." She explained to her that she'd never gotten her anything for her birthday. "And this is why. You've managed to ruin my day with this. This trip would have been the trip of a lifetime."

"No." Justine simply hung up on her. Putting the handle back in the cradle, she was glad once again that she didn't have a cell phone that her sister knew about. If she had, she'd be calling her back in an hour and telling her something else that she'd gotten for her gift from her, and they'd have to start all over again with her telling her no.

She used to have a great deal of trouble telling her sister no. There was a time when she'd go into debt just to pay for whatever she got for herself that she expected her to pay for. Then she'd smartened up. Or nearly became homeless. That was a feeling that she never was having again, to not just be out of work but out of money for even crackers and cheese to eat.

"Did she hit you up?" She told Donald that she'd not been able to tell her what it was, but she was mad. "Good for you. I knew you were smarter than you looked, and you know that I think you're about as ugly as they come."

"Thanks. You date much with that sort of charm?" Donald had been saying the same thing to her since she'd hired him to work in her little restaurant. It had been about the time she'd learned to tell her sister no and to have won one of the largest lotteries that had ever been established. Those three things changed her life for the better, and she had never looked back.

Going back to her office, she finished up with the order she put in and finished up the schedule for the next month. She could do that now that she had established a good working place for people to come to work. Sammy made a habit of hiring people who had only just gotten out of prison for various crimes, mostly white collar. And having a good working environment.

She wouldn't hire abusers, nor would she hire anyone who harmed children. She would run very extensive background checks on everyone, and when it came back with just a hint of abuse on it, she wouldn't hire them. She'd grown up in that kind of setting, and she wasn't going to let anyone in that had hit people.

That's why she didn't understand her sister. Justine had suffered as much as she had at the hands of their parents. More so since she was older. But on a daily basis, they would either be beaten, starved, or both. It was as if their lives were so unimportant to their parents that they could and would forget about them for days on end. Then, when they remembered them, it would be days of daily abuse and starvation, along with mental abuse that nearly destroyed her older sister.

It had taken Justine several years before she'd go out of the house. She was terrified that their parents were going to find them and hurt them. She didn't know what she'd done, but after going to visit her once, she'd not only come out of her home, but she began socializing with others, too. It was such a transformation that she still, to this day, was waiting for her to have a breakdown and do something dangerous to herself.

Once she finished up for the day, she sat in her office and enjoyed her drink. It wasn't often that she'd have ten minutes to herself, and she was going to take advantage of it. As she was leaning back in her chair, her office phone rang. It couldn't be her sister, she didn't have this number, as it was private and no one had it.

"My name is Storm Walsh, and I was wondering if I could have a word with you." She asked her how she got the number. "You know it, so I was able to get it. It wasn't as easy as I thought. You have a very complex mind."

"I don't know what that means, so I'm going to assume that you haven't complimented me. What do you want?" The woman laughed, and she felt her temper flare up. "I'm having my first break since I got out of bed this morning, and you're fucking it up. What do you want, and just so you know, the answer is going to be no. I have no trouble saying that nowadays."

"No, I was just speaking to your sister, and she is upset with you—"

"What do you mean you were just speaking to my sister. Justine has her own life, and if she said I was going to pay for something, she'd be wrong about that, too. So whatever you're selling, I don't want it.

Neither does she." The laughter again, and this time, she found herself smiling. It was the sound of bells. She had no idea why it made her smile, but she did, and it lessened her temper just enough that she could talk to the woman. "Look. Justine has it in her head that I have an endless supply of money. I don't. I have investments as well as other things that my money is going for. Whatever she conned you into, I have nothing to do with it."

"She doesn't know you won the lottery, does she? In fact, no one knows that you won nor that you're the only one that did that week." She asked her how she'd found out. "I told you, when you know something, I can find it. Not as easy as I thought it would be, but it's right there in your mind for me to pick through."

"You've read my mind. I didn't get that the first time you said it. What is it you want? I'm not going to get suckered into a blackmail scheme with you. Whatever you think you know, it's not going to get me to pay you hundreds of thousands of dollars, so you don't tell on me. So state your business, and let me tell you no as well, and we'll end this conversation right now." She told her that she didn't need her money. "That's what everyone says just before they tell you how much they want from you."

"All right, I'm going to get to the point. Several

days ago, there was a man who came into your offices to get hired for a potential job. And in doing so, you were going to do a background check on him. That would have led you straight to me. But he got waylaid and didn't get to see you, so we have to do this the old-fashioned way. I call you. Now. I don't know what was supposed to happen when you hired him. Once he got to your office and met you, you were to go to me, and since that didn't happen for either of us, you didn't get to meet my son, Melbourne. He's your mate." She didn't say anything, thinking that the woman was quite mad. "I'm not mad at all, but a very brilliant woman. I will tell anyone that. But you and Melbourne were to meet, and it didn't happen, and it has to."

"Perhaps the fates decided that I wasn't supposed to meet him after all. Maybe they realized their mistake and decided to waylay him, and they were finished with me and him." Storm said it didn't work that way and that she was indeed supposed to meet him. "Whatever the reason that I didn't, I'm happy for that. I don't want to meet anyone who thinks that I'm going to be their slave forever."

"Why does everyone think that? Has everyone read the same book and come to the conclusion that you have to be a slave to a shifter? I don't know, but I do know that it won't work that way with him. He's a good man, and you two will have a good, long life

together. I promise you I raised him better than that."
Sammy told her good for her. "Yes, and it will be good
for you as well. You must meet him."

"No thanks. See how that worked? I told you
that I'm really good at saying no. I have things in my
life just the way that I want them, and I don't want a
man in my life. I had one of those in my father, and I
don't want to go through that again. You have a nice
day, Storm, and I hope you find someone to pawn your
son off on. It's not going to be me."

Hanging up the phone, she felt really good about
herself. But her break time was over now, and she had
things to do. When her phone rang again, she stepped
out of the office and went about her daily chores at
the restaurant. There were a million and one reasons
she didn't want to talk to Storm again, and only one of
them had to do with her supposed son, who was to be
her mate.

Chapter 1

Sammy finished writing out checks for her employees and put her things away. The safe was the best place for her checkbook and other items for the office, so she knew it would be there when she wanted it. The restaurant was doing very well, and she was happy for it. That meant that all her savings and investments were safe from her having to dig into them because she needed money. It was, for her at least, a win-win situation. She thought about the call that she'd gotten from Storm Walsh and what she said about her being mated to her son. Melbourne was his name, if she remembered correctly.

She gave her this story about how she'd interviewed a man about a position at the restaurant—she only hired convicts, but she did an extensive background test on them so that she could find out if they had any abuse on their records. Neither child nor spousal abuse would be tolerated by her since she'd grown up in that kind of environment when she'd been a child with her sister, Justine. Anyway, she was to have had direct contact with Storm Walsh when she checked this other man's reference, then she'd have contact somehow with Storm's son, Melbourne, and they'd become mates.

For some reason, that didn't happen when it was supposed to, and she wanted to make sure that they still got together. But Sammy didn't want that to happen as she had enough troubles with men, including her father. Storm said that the fates had wanted them to be together for some reason, and Sammy thought that they'd changed their minds about the two of them, and that was fine by her. She didn't want a bossy man in her life at all.

Once she was finished for the day, she made her way home. It was then that she noticed her sister's car out front of her place and dreaded going to the door. Her sister had had a nasty habit of buying herself gifts for her birthday and then expecting Sammy to pay for them. She'd gotten really good at telling her no. If not, her sister would drain her dry of even enough money to buy herself cheese and crackers to get her through the month. She hoped that she'd get it someday, but so far she had to tell her no every year for the last five of them.

About the time she began telling her sister no was when she'd won a jackpot from the lottery. She'd been the only winner, and not only that, but it had been so big that even without all her investments, she would have been able to live a very comfortable life without having to work a single day since then. But she had, it was work or go crazy, so that's what her sister thought she did. Was working as staff for the restaurant when, in actuality, she owned it. Justine knew nothing about her winnings, nor the fact that she owned the restaurant, and she wanted to keep it that way.

"What do you want?" Justine pouted at her and told her she should be nice to her because it was her birthday month. "I've said this to you before, but you're a little too old to be having birthdays for the entire month and expecting me to purchase you something after all this time."

"Why do you have to be so mean to me?" She shrugged her shoulders and said that she made it easy. "I'm coming in, and then we're going to go out to dinner when you change. You're paying."

"No. First off, I'm too tired to want to have to entertain you, and secondly, I have to work in the morning, so going out with you means that I'll be late coming home, and I don't want to do that. Go out and have dinner yourself. Lots of people do that." She said that she never went out to eat on her own. "Well, you're missing out on a great time with yourself, and that's all I have to say about that. Other than again, no, I'm not going out to dinner with you."

"It's the least that you can do since you wouldn't

allow me to buy myself something nice from you. I got my deposit back from your last gift, but they were very testy about it with me." She said she didn't care. "Come on, Sammy. Take me out to dinner. I promise not to beg you for money to get me something. And if you do, I'll allow you to pick out the place we go, so long as it has cloth napkins. I know you're more comfortable with napkins out of a dispenser as well as your food coming out of a Styrofoam box, but I want something nice. It's my birthday today, and I want you to take me out."

"I can pick." She promised her that she wouldn't complain and that it really had to have cloth napkins. "All right. But we leave when we're done eating and not lingering around after until the place closes. I really do have to work tomorrow, and I need to get some sleep."

"Deal." Opening her door, she remembered that she'd not cleaned up after herself this morning when she'd left, as she'd overslept. As her sister chatted on about where she was going to get to go, Sammy went into her bedroom to shower and change. She smelled of food and didn't want the lingering smells to put her off any more than she had to. As soon as she was finished, she met her sister in the living room, where she was watching television.

"You should get yourself a bigger television.

This one is smaller than mine, and while I like the fact that you have something not as nice as I do, I know this thing is from when we were kids and used to watch it in our rooms so that we'd have something to do when we were locked up." Sammy told her sister that it still worked. "Of course it does, it weighs about fifty pounds too. Did you know that they make televisions as thin as a cell phone? What am I talking to you about a cell phone for? You don't have one of those either. You must be the only person in the world who has a house phone to use."

"I doubt that. And besides, I really don't need to be bothered by the phone when I'm home. It makes it so that I can get a good night's sleep for a change." Justine huffed at her, and she had to laugh. It would be like her to think that she doesn't have anything to do with the twentieth century. "Are you ready to go? I am. Remember the rules, Justine, or I'll leave you with the bill when I walk out."

The restaurant was nice, and the food was good and solid. She ordered what she wanted, not worrying about the calories, while Justine fussed about everything being full of carbs. After clearing her throat for the second time, she ordered and gave her menu to the waiter. Then she glared at her.

"I should have known that you'd take me to a place like this." She asked her what was wrong with it. "Everything is so Italian. Next time that I make a bargain like this with you, I'm going to insist on it being a place that has no pasta."

"Make too many stipulations and I'll pass on taking you out. I love it here. It's a calming place, the staff is really good, and you can get all the salad you want. If you wanted no carbs, I know that the salad here is good for you. It's why I love this place so much." She huffed again, and Sammy decided to ignore her for the people sitting around them.

She loved places where people were. She didn't care for dealing with them all the time, but she did enjoy listening to them as they talked around their table. Sometimes she'd get a bit of gossip, other times she would figure out why she didn't like dealing with people. Sammy thought that all men and women were selfish and rude to others. Just like her parents were.

"I saw Dad the other day. He's looking old." She turned to look at Justine. "He was coming out of the hardware store. It looked more like he was being thrown out, but I didn't hang around to see what that was about."

"You need to be more careful. What if he'd had seen you? Or Mom? What would you have done then?" She said that she was forever careful not to be around them, that's why she saw him. She'd been making sure he wasn't around her. "They're dangerous, you know.

And won't hesitate to hurt you if they can get to you."

"I know that better than you do." She nodded and asked her if she'd seen their mom. "No. Not to say that she wasn't hanging around him, too, but I saw him and left the area. I was terrified that he was going to see me. I thought for sure that he'd be dead by now."

"One can only hope, Justine." She filled her plate with salad when it arrived at their table. She noticed that Justine had done the same to her plate. "What are you doing hanging around a hardware store anyway? I thought that you had a handyman at your place who does all the repairs."

"I wasn't at the hardware store, but walking by it. I needed to get something for my washer. Did you know that you're supposed to wash your washer once in a while to keep it in good working order? Dumbest thing I ever saw, but I read up on it yesterday, and they say that's true. It also keeps your clothing from staining too much or something like that." Sammy told her that she had nothing to do with the washer and dryer at her apartment complex. "You still share with the others in your place? That's just gross, Sammy. When I moved this last time, I made sure that I had my own hookup for a washer and dryer. I wanted to be safe when I went to wash my clothing. And it's nice to have my own set when I think about how many germs are going through the ones there. You should think about moving into my place. They have a lot of rules, but they take care of me when I need it."

"I have no intentions of moving anytime soon. I've lived there for the last ten years and I'm going to be living there for the next ten." After getting a second bowl of salad, she declined the breadsticks. She thought that they were all right, but she didn't care for them on the whole. She wasn't a bread eater to begin with. "What's going to happen to you this winter, as you no longer have a car? I thought that you liked driving everywhere."

"I hated having to keep up with the rules all the time. And twice, the condo place that I'm living in said that I was to be fined if I parked my car illegally again. It's cheaper for me to have someone drive me around than it was for me to keep a car. Without having to pay for insurance, I save myself money for as much as I use the driving service that is part of the place I live. They even go to the grocery store once a month so that I can hitch a ride on one of the buses they use." She told her that would get old fast. "Not for me. I love not having to worry about things like that. It's just one more thing to get in the way when I'm trying to do something. I kept forgetting where I parked my car and had to walk home anyway, so this is saving me the heartache."

Once their dinners were brought to them, it was Justine who suggested they have desserts before they left. Since she never counted calories or bothered with carbs, Sammy said it was fine by her. She could take it home and eat it tomorrow for breakfast if she was too full to enjoy it tonight. However, once they were finished with their dinner, they both had room for some of the cheesecake that they had in store. It was a great ending to a nice evening out with her sister.

"I had fun tonight." She told Justine that she'd had fun as well and was glad that she'd bullied her into it. "You blackmailed me, but I find that I'm all right with that tonight. Thank you for dinner, little sister."

"You're so very welcome, big sister." They parted ways at the restaurant parking lot and made their way to their homes. Neither one lived far from the place, which was one of the reasons she'd thought of it, and it was a perfect night for walking home. Just as she was leaving the lot, she saw her parents as they were sorting through the dumpster at the place they'd only just eaten at. Looking around for Justine, to make sure she was safe, Sammy hid behind one of the larger trees on the lot and made sure they couldn't see her.

Sammy had left home one night when she was sixteen years old. Justine had stayed; she couldn't get her to leave home for any amount of persuasion. To this day, she still didn't know what had happened to her sister when her parents were released from jail. When the two of them had been put in prison for eight and a half years, later that same year, Justine had stayed at the house like she was still terrified that they'd come home and find her gone. That was when she made a life for herself without them around. It took Justine another five years of never leaving the house — with her bringing her food and water to live off of, before she finally left. The house was torn down the following year because of gentrification going on in the neighborhood. It was the best thing that had ever happened to the street that they'd grown up on, if anyone were to ask her.

When her parents moved on, obviously finding something to eat in the dump, she made her way carefully to her home. She didn't know what they'd do to her after all this time, but she wasn't going to take the chance of her having to find out either. Having them out of her life made it so much better than it was even as a child. Sammy didn't care if they were her parents; she didn't like them at all and had no respect for them either.

Once she was home, she locked up and began sorting her own laundry. Her sister had never ventured beyond her living room, not even to go into the kitchen when she was over. But Sammy not only had a washer and dryer set of her own, she had also read up on the washing of her washer and did it when it was time. Sammy loved just what her sister said about washing her own clothing, to not have to share her things, but she also liked being able to know that her things hadn't been rooted through while she was gone from them. Putting in the last load, she was ready for bed when her house phone rang.

"It's Storm again. I have a question for you. I've asked you this before, but does your sister know that you won the lottery? Or that you own the complex where you live?" She asked her why it should matter to her. "Because I'm trying to make you distracted while my son goes to your door. I'm afraid I can't wait for the fates to try again. He knows what you are to him and is slightly pissed off at me because I told him."

Her front doorbell rang, and she was just pissed enough to hang up on the other woman. But she kept her on the line so that she could hear what she had to say to her son. She wasn't slightly pissed but royally pissed off and didn't care who knew it. Opening the door for him, she was surprised to see not just him but her parents were on the sidewalk right outside the door. Dragging him in and shutting the door, she looked out the peephole to see if they had noticed her standing in the doorway. They didn't seem to know she was right there, and now she had to contend with a man that she didn't want in her life.

"Is everything all right?" She kept watching for her parents when she told him no, everything wasn't all right. "I'm sorry to barge in like this…Well, that's not what happened; you dragged me in here. I'm assuming that you don't want the people to know that you live here."

"They're my parents, and you assumed correctly." She turned and looked at him as he made his way to her couch. "Don't get too comfy here. I'm tossing you right out as soon as I know that they're gone."

"My mom sent me here. While I don't care for the way she put the two of us together, it sounds to me like you need someone to protect you. Will they hurt you if they find you?" She said she didn't want to give them the chance of hurting her. "I understand that. If it helps you any at all, you're immortal from the moment that you touched me."

"Why would that be helpful to know that I can't die from them? I'm betting that I can still be hurt, however." He said that was true, but hurting wasn't dead, and he thought that she'd like that. "I don't know what to do about them hanging around. This is the second time I've seen them tonight, and I don't like it. And what did I tell you about getting comfy around my place?"

"This is a very comfy couch. I bet the chairs are too." He got up to test his theory about them and smiled at her. "They are, aren't they? Where did you get them? When we get a house, you're picking out the furniture so that we can have comfy stuff in the living room." Rolling her eyes at him, she looked out the door again to see if they were out there. When she didn't see them, she relaxed a bit, but then realized that she'd have to deal with the man. "Melbourne. That's my name. Melbourne Walsh. You've spoken to my mom."

"She's very pushy." He laughed like that was an understatement or something. "Did she give you the long version of what happened as to why we didn't meet?"

"Yes, she told me about the interview that you had in your place." He looked good sitting on her chair and decided that she'd had enough excitement for one night. She needed to go to bed. "I only came to meet you and to see where you lived. This is a nice place but a little cramped, don't you think?"

"What I think is that it's time you went home. And don't come back." He pouted, and she found that she wanted to suckle his lower lip into her own mouth to see if it tasted as good as she thought that it might. When that thought entered her head, she decided that she was more tired than she thought she was and stood up to have him leave. "I really have a long day tomorrow, and I need to get into my bed. Alone."

"I'm not going to bother you at work, but my mom told me where you work right now. It's very commendable that you hire ex-cons to work for you to give them a much-needed hand up in the world." She said it was time for him to go again. "I'm leaving, but I wanted you to know that if you ever need me, you need only to think of me, and we can talk. We have a link that only the two of us share."

"Why would I want to talk to you?" He said that she could be in trouble. "I'm forever getting myself out of one mess or another. It's what I live for. But don't hold your breath in looking for me to contact you. I don't need anyone in my life at the moment. I have enough going on as it is." He said that he'd reach out to her when he needed her then. "Whatever floats your boat. As I said, I'm a very busy person who doesn't like to hang on the phone at all. Nor do I want your mind tricks."

When he left, she finished her last load of laundry and went to her bedroom. She put her things aside for her to wear tomorrow and made her way to her bed. Sammy was a sound sleeper and could fall asleep in a moment, but tonight she tossed and turned. She knew that it had a lot to do with seeing her parents tonight, but didn't know for sure. It could have been the big man who had invaded her home, too.

Finally getting up before the alarm went off, she put her clothing in the dryer and made herself some breakfast. It was only a bowl of cereal, but it would be something on her belly, and that was all she was looking for right now. Making sure to check the peephole once again, she was out the door and into her car in a few moments without seeing her parents.

No one at work knew she was the owner of the restaurant. She thought perhaps Donald, her cook, had guessed it, but since he never asked, she didn't tell him. He'd been working for her since she opened, and they'd become friends. Not good friends, but friends all the same. She loved his sense of humor, and he liked her no-nonsense way of dealing with things.

~*~

Melbourne couldn't believe his luck. Not only had he found his mate—with his mother's help—but he'd figured out that she was as bad or good, depending on how he looked at it, as the other women in his family. He loved the fact that she was going to be a ballbuster. So long as she didn't take her frustrations out on him.

As he made his way back to his home, he decided to keep an eye out for the couple that had scared his mate. He had noticed them enough to know how to pick them out; it wasn't difficult to do that when they stunk of body odor and were dressed in clothing that had seen better days. Seeing them twice more, he had a feeling that while they were out searching for something—more than likely food, they didn't seem to be looking for Sammy. He wondered just for a moment if her name was Sammy or Samantha. Not that it mattered, but it was something else that he didn't know about her.

He did know a great deal more about her than she did of him, he was sure. All of it thanks to his mom and her not trusting anyone. She'd done a background check on her when she'd first found out that she was his mate, and he didn't know yet if he was all right with that. He was sure that she'd done it on the other mates, but he was no less upset that she'd done it on his mate before he met her.

Just as he was getting out of his car at his place, he heard from his brother Dyson. Emma was working today, and he was bored. Telling him that he'd meet him for lunch later on had him wondering what he was doing now.

"I'm going to work on some projects for the family. I have two contracts to go over, as well as I have to inspect a building downtown before we buy it, and find out it wasn't worth it later. Why?" He told him that he'd help him with the inspection, as he really was bored out of his mind with his mate gone. "You should have a couple of kids or something. That should keep you out of trouble."

"No it won't. I'll just be hanging out with you guys while I drag my kids around with me. You'd love it. Being an uncle to my kids. Someday soon, I'm going to be a daddy and you'll be so jealous." He told him that he'd beat him in getting his mate with child. "You have to find her first, don't you? I mean, that's the way that it works."

"I did find her. She and I met just tonight. Mom told me about her, and I went to see what she's like. You're going to love her, she's just like the others." He asked him why he hadn't announced it to everyone yet. "We just met, and I'm making sure that she and I get off to a better start than the rest of you guys did. Fowler really messed up, and I don't plan on doing anything like he did."

Fowler, his oldest brother, had assumed that he was going to have to train Amy to be a good woman to be around. Not only that, but he had it in his thick head that she was going to want all his money, too. Not only had she saved him from certain death by reattaching his head when Grail had tried to remove it, but he'd had to save Amy from being killed by their great-grandma when she was set to remove her head.

Grail was a dragon, the same as mom and they were. However, Grail was into black magic, and it had turned his dragon black as the magic he was using. One night when Fowler was feeling sorry for himself and out on his own, Grail snuck up behind him and removed his head, but for a one-inch flap of skin that held his head onto his shoulders. Amy had killed

Grail, then set Fowler's head back on his shoulders so that he could heal. If not for that small flap of skin, Fowler would have surely been killed, and they would never have found out what their great-grandma had had plans for them all.

"Come on, let me go with you. If I call out to Emma again today, she's going to brain me, and that won't be pretty. I'll even do most of the work for you." He suggested that he go inspect the building while he did the contracts. "I can do that. But I'd rather hang out with you instead. That way, as soon as we're done, we can go have lunch together and you can tell me all about your mate."

"All right, but I have those contracts to look over, and you can't be pestering me while I'm doing it. I'll brain you and I'll make sure that your pretty face isn't anything that Emma ever wants to look at again. Promise me that you'll behave yourself." He promised that he'd be as good as gold. "Good. I don't have time for you messing with me when I have to get them finished up. Then I want to go and see what kind of trouble I can get into with my mate. She's beautiful and I want to get to know her."

"I promise I'll be good." He could tell that his brother wasn't going to be helpful or good, but he was sort of keeping him from finding his mate right now and asking her all the questions that were going around in his head. He wanted to know all about her and her comfy furniture. "If you give me one of the contracts, we can get them finished sooner."

In the end, he did give his brother one of the contracts to read over. He knew where they were from; the city was asking for funding for two new cruisers for the town. One of them had been in an accident late last year, and the second one was just worn out. The contract that he was reading over was for new baseball fields put in this fall, so that by the time spring rolled around, there would be better grounds for the kids to play on. He was excited about that as he'd played ball on the same fields when he'd been a teenager.

"I suggest that mom and dad have a look at the new cars they want and maybe buy used. There is so little crime in his area that I don't see a need for something that will get speeds of over a hundred miles per hour. For the price of one car, they can get two used ones, and that would suit the town better." He agreed with his brother and then asked about the baseball fields. "We just put in the football fields this past fall. I don't know that they need all the fields replaced so much as they need them to be redone. Replacing seems like a great deal more work than just having the fields leveled out and redone. Maybe that would be a project for five years down the line. Or not. It might save money by getting it done now and not having to do it in five or so years. That's a close call."

"I think it would save time and money to just get it finished up and upgraded. The way the fields are looking now, someone could get hurt with all the kids who play on the fields. Plus, with the added money that we'll be putting in, we can have four fields laid instead of only the two, and that will save the kids from having to play late in the evening when they have a double header. I remember playing some of those until it was too dark to see. Even the lights didn't help all that much when it was nine o'clock when we finished up." Dyson said he liked that idea much better. "I do as well. Especially when it comes to getting four fields instead of just the two that we have now. I hope mom and dad like the idea."

After writing up their ideas on the contracts for the city, the two of them went to the building on Main Street to have a look. His first thought was that it was in good enough shape for what they wanted it for, but upon closer inspection, getting into the basement and attic of the thing, they both thought that the building needed to be torn down and started over. It was in such bad shape. Not only would they have to tear it down, but he thought that using it as a training building for the fire department might be a terrible idea, as it might well fall on them, too. Yes, he thought that tearing the building down would be safer for all those concerned.

They headed to lunch after letting their parents know their decision on the building.

"I'm hungry for a sub." Dyson loved double meat subs from the ice cream place just down the road from where the building had been. "How about we have two subs each and finish it off with a banana split each?"

"Sounds good." Just as he was sitting down, he could feel the first touches of someone trying to reach out to him. He didn't know why, but he thought immediately that it was Sammy and that she had changed her mind about needing him. But he realized that she was stressed, and he waited for her to get in touch with him. When she didn't, he asked her if things were all right.

"Not really. We're being robbed." He was just standing up to go to her when she told him that she had it. "It's never happened here before, and my employees are freaking out. How do I calm them down?"

"You need to be calm, and they'll take their cues from you. Just project a feeling that you've done this before and they'll be just fine." He hesitated for just a second. "I'm going to come to you, but I've only just realized that I have no idea where you are. Can you give me an address?"

"Yes." She told him, but also told him to be careful, as they were armed. "I'll be as careful as I can be. You're my mate, and I need to protect you."

"I don't even know what you are." He told her that he was a large, mean-looking dragon. "By large, I'm assuming that if you were to shift in my restaurant, then there wouldn't be anything left of it."

"You'd be right." He thought of her stress level and decided to help her out with that. "I don't think I've ever been robbed at my place of business before. I've been robbed before when I was out and about. They got about two hundred dollars from me."

It was more like they got five grand, but he didn't want her to freak out when that was the amount he had on him. People didn't carry that much cash on them when they were only walking about normally. As he spoke to her, he made his way to the restaurant where she was working. It wasn't that far; it was a place that he'd never tried before. And he told her that.

"We have good food and a great staff. The man is demanding that we all get into the cooler, except for me. I have to open the safe for him. He should have timed it better. I only just got back from the bank. All that's in the safe is about two hundred dollars, which is in each of the two drawers." Melbourne suggested that she didn't tell him that. "I won't. But had he been in here two hours ago, he would have gotten nearly ten grand. Are you coming here by chance? I could use you, I think."

"I'm standing outside the restaurant now. When he comes out, I'll nab him with the police and you'll get your money back." She told him to be careful, and he promised her that he would. "But you'll owe us lunch. My brother and I were just getting ready to order some when you reached for me."

"Deal. You said that the cops were with you? How did you get them there so fast?" He told her that he had a buddy on the force, and he knew when he called for him, he needed him. "Good. I'll have to remember that if I ever get robbed again."

He felt her pain, and he also felt his dragon shifting under his skin. Before he could ask her if she was all right, she told him that he'd hit her for not paying attention to him. She'd been talking to him and had missed what he said.

"He'll be lucky if he makes it to jail for hitting you." She told him that she was fine but paying attention to him now. "I'm sorry. That was all my fault." She told him that he was leaving now.

It was over the moment he came out of the back door. Lucky for the man, he'd not been at the back door but the front one waiting for him. Dyson popped him in the head, and down he went. The police had him handcuffed before he could make it back there to teach him a lesson on how to treat his mate.

Everyone was all right but for the head wound

on Sammy's head. It wasn't that bad, not as bad as it could have been, but she went to the hospital to make sure she was all right. The police told her that she needed to make it look good for the prosecutor when it came to trial anyway. She even told the staff to make sure that the two of them were fed before they left. Melbourne went to the hospital with her to calm his beast.

After she was seen in the emergency department, he called his brother Edgar to make sure that everyone at the restaurant was all right. He said that he could do that for him, as he was out that way anyway, and was glad to do it for him. It was Tabby who got back with him to tell him that she had been with Edgar and that everyone was having a good time being closed up and writing out their reports as to what had happened.

"They're all relieved that they made it through the robbery. They seem to think that it was your mate, whom I didn't know you'd found, that saved them all from being hurt. She'd been so calm." He said that was what got her popped in the head, her talking to him to calm her. "Well, you impressed everyone here. They'll be singing your praises for years to come, I'm betting."

After Sammy's head was X-rayed, they said she could have something for pain. She was going to need a few stitches, but he didn't think it would come to that. She was already healing from her wound thanks to her being his mate. When she made it back to the little room she was in, he held her hand, and he was surprised when she let him.

"Don't get used to this." He swore that he'd not. "Good. I'm just nervous, that's all, and you calm me down for some reason. Is that a mate thing?"

"It is. There will be more magic coming to you as well. You should be able to change your clothing at will. You might even be able to bring things to you. That's what the other women can do." She asked him what else she might get. "I don't know, to be honest with you. It's different for each mate. Amy can bounce in flames, which only takes her seconds to get somewhere. All the others have their own kind of unique magic that came from being mates to our dragons."

"Will I be able to shift? Not that I'd look forward to that, but it would be something that comes in handy." He said that sadly, none of the women could shift, but that didn't mean she wouldn't be able to. "I guess I'll have to try it. Why did you come to me when I was being robbed? I mean, you could have just called the police."

"I needed to know that you were all right. My sole purpose in life now is to keep you safe and happy. I'm not saying that I won't mess up sometimes, but I will live my life around you and making you safe.

That means your sister, too. You have one, right?" She said that she did, but she was older than her by twelve years. "I'm older than both of you by centuries. I've been around for a long time. And my mother, since the beginning of time. She and my aunt, along with all of us, are time shifters. They keep the world from having a disaster when there might be people who are needed later down the line. They make sure that there are no blips of any kind so that people, humans mostly, don't know what the world is doing at any given time."

"Wow." He didn't know if she believed him or not, but let it go. She'd find out soon enough when she met the rest of his family. "My family doesn't have much to say for itself. My parents were abusive toward Justine and me all our lives, and they would starve us, too, as if they had forgotten that we were around. There were times that we barely made it, but it's not for them ending up in jail for long periods of time; we might not have. Lucky for us, the two of us were resourceful in making sure we could find something to eat and keep us healthy. They were in prison for a while, and that's how we were able to move on without them. I don't know if they're looking for us or not, but I'm not taking any chances with them. I've had enough abuse for one lifetime."

They talked until she was released to go home and put her feet up. As soon as the doctor told her what to do, Melbourne knew that she'd not do it. It was all he could do to keep her from going back to work right as they were leaving. He told her that she'd have to change her clothing at the very least. She did so with her magic.

"Now that's what I call a handy thing to have." He said that he loved it as well. It had kept him from wearing dusty clothing to her restaurant when she'd called for him. "I didn't mean to take you from your work. I was just scared and scared for the people that work for me. They were stressing out and making me stressed out. Thanks for keeping me calm like you did."

"It was my pleasure." Taking her to her home so that she could get her laptop, he got a better view of her home. It was a little two-bedroom condo that held a certain charm for him. She had decorated it with all the earthtones that she could find, and he found it to be the most calming room he'd ever been in. He especially loved the chairs she had in her living room. "I'll take you back to work and then hang around for a little while. I promise you I won't get in your way, but I was wondering if we could have dinner tonight. I'd love to be able to get to know you better."

"You say that now, but I'm betting that once you do get to know me, you'll wish you hadn't. Like I said, I'm not much of anything when I was talking about my family." He told her that he'd be the judge of that. "Suit yourself, but don't say I didn't warn you."

"I'm fine with getting to know everything I can about you. Even the stuff that you've buried so deep that you've forgotten about it." She laughed, and he knew in that moment that he'd fallen in love with his pretty mate. She laughed like she meant it and didn't care who heard her. He loved her for that. "I'll pick you up at six, and we can have a nice dinner, then walk around town while having some ice cream."

"Very adult-sounding until you got to the ice cream." He laughed with her and decided to get out of her place before he became too comfy again. He didn't want to piss her off because he wanted to take a nap in her chair. Besides, he had plenty to do this afternoon to keep him busy, even if one of his other brothers hung out with him to annoy him. "I'll see you tonight then. Thanks again for keeping me safe and calm during the robbery."

He drove home when he dropped her off at her restaurant. He loved the name of it, The Morning Dew, and thought that he could have breakfast there every morning. But he'd not, not right away. He wanted to not annoy her while trying to get to know her. Melbourne was going to romance his mate until she fell in love with him, then he'd double his efforts when she said she did. Loving her was going to be easy, and he couldn't wait to get to know every part of her mind and, of course, her body.

Chapter 2

Rachel didn't want to be caught by Daniel again. The last time, it was five years ago, he had nearly killed her. But Grandma said that he was in jail and she was counting on that. She saw Melbourne just as he was pulling into her grandmother's driveway. Without his help, she might well have missed her grandma even more and her little boy, Danny.

Disappearing like she had, had caused her grandma to worry. All she'd been doing was going out for formula and diapers for Danny when he'd been a baby and never returned. It had hurt her like she'd never been hurt to leave the two most important people in her life, but it was that or be killed. She was nearly caught unawares, like she had been that day.

Daniel had never cared for Danny, so that wasn't an issue for her grandma. She knew that he was in good hands, and the man that she was staying with, Mr. Gross, had been pretending to take his picture so that he could show it to his dead wife when he went to the cemetery. When all along he'd been bringing the pictures to her so that she could see her son grow up. It had been five years since she saw him close up enough to touch him, and even longer than that since she'd been able to get a hug from him.

"I was just coming to tell your grandma that Daniel's court hearing is in the morning. I should have told her sooner, but I kept getting waylaid. My mate found me." She hugged him and told him congratulations on his happiness. "Yes, we're only just now getting to know one another, so we have things to work out. But I also want to be there for you and your little family. Daniel is facing prison time for knocking over that mail box and then urinating on the mail that had fallen out of it. This was no accident that happened, but malicious tampering with the mail."

"Mr. Gross has been keeping me updated on things going on around town. I'm so glad that I was able to stay with him when Daniel found me that last time. If not for him, I don't even want to think about what might have happened to me." Melbourne said he was happy that he was able to help, too. "Grandma is singing your praises about how you found me when I was hiding across the street from her. It afforded me to be able to see Danny once in a while when he was waiting for the bus or playing in her yard."

"I'm happy that this will soon be over." She was as well and said as much to the big man. All the Walsh men were big men, and she was glad for it. "I can pick you and your grandma up in the morning. My mom said she'd watch over Danny. There isn't any reason for him to be in the courtroom to hear what he's going to say."

"None of it will be nice, I'm sure." Rachel thanked him for the ride, and the two of them went into her grandma's home. It was one of the nicest homes on the street, and she was ever so proud of her grandma for doing all that she had done to keep Danny safe and going to school. "Are you staying for dinner, Mr. Melbourne?"

"No, I have a date tonight." He told Grandma about finding his mate, and she told him how happy she was for him as well. "We're just getting to know one another right now. She and I have only been around each other for the last few days, and I'm already in love with her."

"Of course you are. And she couldn't be getting a better mate than you." His cheeks pinked up when Grandma said that to him, and she had to hide her smile. For such a large man, he was embarrassed easily.

After giving them all the information on Daniel's trial, he went home. The man was very nice for keeping them informed about the trial and such, and she couldn't believe that it was nearly over with Daniel. Once he was in prison, she'd be free to move back into her grandma's home and take over the care of her son. Her grandma was very sick, and the doctors hadn't given her much longer to live, which was another reason she'd gone to Melbourne to find her. He had an uncanny ability to touch something or someone, and that would lead him right to them. It was how he'd found her when Grandma had asked.

After Melbourne left them, they settled into making dinner. Danny would be home from preschool soon, and she couldn't wait to see him. She knew that Daniel's mother lived next door to her grandma and was telling Daniel all kinds of things about her. Rachel found that she didn't care about the old bitty and hoped that she would go to jail with her son. There had to be some kind of law that would have her put away for spying on people. She knew that there wasn't, but she thought that there should be. It would be worth it to tell on her for a change.

Just as they were sitting down to dinner, the three of them, Mr. Gross came over to let them know that the trial was tomorrow too. She told him that Melbourne had already told them, and he was invited to have dinner with them. Rachel owed that man her life and that of her grandma, too, for all the things that he'd been doing for her.

"Do you know what you're going to be doing once Daniel is in prison? I mean, you can still work from home as you've been doing, so that won't be a problem." She told her grandma that she was going to get to know her son a bit more for sure. "You've missed a lot of years. I just wish I'd have gone to that young man earlier to find you. Maybe things would have been different for the three of us."

"I didn't miss a lot of years of just Danny growing up, Grandma, but you being there for me too. You understand why I didn't come home, don't you? I mean, especially with Ms. Crow living right next door to you. There is no telling what might have happened if he had found me at the Gross house. He would have killed you, too."

"Yes, he's always been a bad person. Even as a child, he was never one that anyone could trust with any of their toys when the kids were out in the yard playing. Why I remember one time he took your dolly and ran over her with the lawn mower. His parents didn't do anything but say that he was a boy. That's why he's so mean nowadays, they never blistered his ass when he needed it."

"That's for sure. He didn't mess with my boys when they got old enough to shift. I think he was afraid of Opal, too. Here she was just a little bitty thing, and he was terrified of her. Should have been beaten more as a kid. You're right about that." Mr. Gross had four children, and Opal was his only girl. They were all shifter wolves like she and Danny were. "Yes, sir, he was terrified of my little girl, and I was never so happy to see him get his comeuppance as I was the day he thought that he could mess with her. I still laugh about how she tore into him and ripped his pants nearly off of him that day."

Daniel had caught Opal alone in the yard while she was playing with her dolls. He'd come up behind her, startling the little girl enough that she shifted long before she was supposed to. Once she had done that, she'd chased him all the way to his house and around the yard a few times until he could get inside. His momma never said a word to Mr. Gross, either, even though Daniel had had to have several stitches to heal up. Daniel never set foot in their yard after that.

She helped her son with his alphabet before he was given his bath and readied for bed. It was calming for her to be able to do that, and she thought that it helped her grandma, too. She was sick, and it was beginning to show on her daily. It broke her heart that her grandma had been told she had cancer. Nasty disease that was, and she'd not wish it on anyone. Not even Daniel, for as much as she hated him.

Cleaning up the kitchen after Mr. Gross left, she sat down at the table and thought about her life so far. She was only twenty-six years old and felt on some days that she was older than her grandma. Feeling sorry for herself had never been anything that she did, but tonight was getting her down because of something that Danny had asked her. He asked her if she was going to leave him again.

"Not for all the money in the world will I leave you again." He hugged her tightly after that, and she felt her eyes fill with tears. As soon as he was in bed, he asked for a pinky promise that she'd stay, and she gave it to him. "I love you, little man, and I will no matter what happens."

Going to bed when her grandma did, she lay awake trying to decide if she should go tomorrow or not. She was afraid if she was honest with herself. Not just of Daniel getting off from his deeds, but that he'd get away from the police and somehow hurt her badly. That nightmare had been haunting her since she'd woken up one morning five years ago in a hospital room far from her home and her son.

Getting up the next morning, she was ready to go when her grandma was. True to his word, a car was sent for her and her grandma, and they were at the courthouse in plenty of time to get a seat. They sat with all the Walsh family, and it made her feel better about everything with them there. They were dragons she knew and wished that one of them could gobble Daniel up, and they'd be done with him. But that wasn't to be, she knew that and watched as the proceedings began in the trial.

"All rise." She knew that she had to pay

attention now so she'd not mess things up, but she missed the name of the judge who was presiding over things today. When Daniel was brought out, she almost didn't recognize him. He'd gotten fat, and his hair was nearly all gone. If not for the judge saying his name, she was sure that she would have thought that there was someone else in the room with them. Grandma held her hand as they listened to the charges against Daniel.

He was being tried by a federal judge because he'd destroyed a few mailboxes. She'd thought it was just the one, but there were five of them. Melbourne had told her that each one of them was a two-hundred and fifty thousand dollar fine or up to three years in prison if found guilty, or both. Then there was the crime of urinating on the mail that had been in the mailboxes. She might well be away from him while he was in prison for a lot longer if things went the way that she hoped they did.

There were video cameras from homes that showed him destroying the mailboxes. Even video of him urinating on some of the mail, too. Once it was established that he'd committed the crime, there was the sentencing phase of today. He was asked if he had any questions or concerns before his sentencing.

"I didn't know that that was a crime, your honor." He told him that it was written right there on the mailboxes. "Well, I didn't see it. Perhaps they should make it in bigger print so that everybody can see it. The next time I have myself a fit, I'll be sure not to touch the mailboxes. Just fine me and that's all you need to do. I've learned my lesson for that."

"You think that you'll be able to afford over a million dollars in fines, Mr. Crow? That's the rate that it's going to cost you." He said he didn't have that kind of money on him at the moment. "Are you being an ass in my courtroom, sir? I surely hope not. You either pay the fine or I'm going to put you in prison for the maximum number of years I can give you. Twenty years is a long time to think about what you did."

"I've already been in jail for six months." The attorney for the government said it had only been two and a half months. "Seems like a lot longer to me. Just give me something for good behavior, and we can call it a day. I don't have that kind of money, and I doubt anyone does."

"You should have thought of that before you messed with the mailboxes and the mail within them." He said that he'd think on that real hard, but he'd already lost his job and needed to find his wife. "Your ex-wife, you mean. She divorced you nearly three years ago."

"I've been looking for her since before that. She's got my son, and while I don't care about him,

I do want to get her back to the house and take care of me. It's not fair that she could divorce me when I couldn't find hide nor hair of her. You find her and tell her she needs to pay those fines; it's the least she can do for leaving me like she did." He looked around the room and right over her. "She should be here since she is the one who caused me to have my temper flare up like it did. If she'd just have been home when I got there, then none of this would have happened to me."

"It says here that you beat her daily, sometimes causing her to go to the hospital. Is that right?" He said a man had to keep his wife in line. "That's against the law too, were you aware of that?" He waved him off like it wasn't anything that he wanted to be concerned with. "I don't know what that means. You'll have to use your words when in my courtroom, young man."

"As I said, you have to be able to keep them in line. And if they need it so bad as they end up in the hospital, then that should be a lesson that they learned." She knew that he thought that he was right, but hearing him say the words out loud really made her think what a monster he'd been to her all those years. "What do you say we get this over with, and I can go on with my life. I've wasted enough time in that poor excuse for a jail as it is. Just let me off for good behavior, and that'll be the end of my time here."

He was sentenced to not just the twenty-one

years in prison, but he also had to work at the prison to pay back the fines that he incurred while on his crime spree. She wanted to get up and dance, but was afraid that he'd see her and come after her. Even with all the officers in the room, she wasn't stupid enough to think that he'd not be able to get to her.

~*~

Melbourne was happy with the results of the trial. It had been quickly taken care of because Daniel had become such a problem in jail. Not taking a bath was only one of a dozen or so issues they were having with him. Another one was his whining all the time about things, like food, and his not being able to watch television.

Going to see Sammy at work, he decided that he was going to see if she could have lunch with him while there. He normally wouldn't do anything like that, but he had a list of questions to ask her about getting them a home and land that he could take care of for them.

He was excited about having a home like his brothers. He really didn't know what kind of house he wanted; he'd leave that up to Sammy, but he wanted to have some land that he could shift and lie on when he could. Going to the other realm was fine for him at times, but he did want his own land so that he could take care of the grounds, too. Planting things, flowers, and trees was high on his list of things to do. Someday, he wanted to see his kids playing in his yard, too. If Sammy wanted to have any, that was.

"I can't have lunch with you until after the lunch rush." He said that he could wait for her, and she looked frustrated. "I'm going to have to clear tables and be hostess. I have two people who called off today. And while I'm all right with working here, it's going to be a lot to get done."

"I can buss tables. I've done it before." She said she couldn't ask him to do that. "You didn't ask, I said I'd do it. I don't mind at all. It'll give me something to do while I wait for you. It'll be fun too." He asked for an apron and was given one. There were already several tables that needed to be cleaned off, and he was ready to get to it. "I'll take them to the kitchen and work like that. I don't mind at all to help you out."

He worked for nearly three hours straight without a break and thought that he was having the best time ever. It was busy, as soon as he cleared a table, Sammy was seating someone in the cleaned space. The staff seemed to be having a good time, too, and showed him how to set up the tables so that they could save time. Putting the silverware on the table with napkins was easy for him since he was already there in the first place.

When things started to slow down around two-thirty, he was shown how to put tablecloths on the tables that were no longer in a rush to be used. As soon as he put the tablecloth on the tables, it gave the room a brighter appeal. When he took back the last of the bus tubs, the kitchen was very helpful in showing him how to stack things so that they could get to the dishes quicker. He loved the way that things had a flow, and he was more than happy to do what they needed to get things cleaned up faster. He went to find Sammy when one of the dishwasher workers told him she was looking for him.

"You did a fantastic job. I've never had tables turn so quickly before. Makes me realize how much James is screwing off." He said he'd not meant to get anyone in trouble. "It's fine. James has been complaining about how much work he has to do and doesn't get any respect. I think that the waitstaff is thrilled to have their tables turned so quickly. It means more tips for them."

"Speaking of tips, they tried to give me part of theirs. I don't need the money, and I really enjoyed myself." She said she'd have to pay him something. "Buy me lunch and we'll be even. And I mean it when I say that if you run short again, give me a call. I'll gladly come and help you out again."

"What about for dinner?" He was sitting in the dining room with her now, and the place was empty but for the two of them. "When James called off, I didn't realize it was for the night shift as well. If you could help us out again, I'd be very grateful."

"Gladly." He ate the food that was set in front of him. "I've been seeing this on a lot of tables when I went by. This looks great." He ate more than half of his lunch before she'd been able to give him his drink. "I guess I was hungrier than I thought. And I love that I'm getting to have lunch with you, too."

The two of them enjoyed their lunch of hamburgers and fries. He had a milkshake with, and she had a bottle of water. When they were finished, two of the waitstaff came over and thanked him again for working today, and they made a lot of tips because of him. He told them that he had a good time and was going to be doing it tonight, too. They were both thrilled and told the other two waitresses who were filling salt shakers and folding napkins around silverware.

"This place runs well. And with all the little things you have in place, I can see where they enjoy getting things out faster. I was amazed at the amount of business that you do here as well." She said normally they didn't have that sort of business, but because he'd been able to get the tables cleaned off, they all had a good day. "I'm glad that I could help. I'm guessing since you're short-staffed tonight that our dinner date is canceled."

"I'm sorry. I forgot all about it when they called

off. I think I'm going to have to fire them both because this is the third time this week that they've called off. And on a Friday afternoon, too, is a big no-no around here. They know that we're busy. It's payday for most of the people around here, and going out to lunch is a big deal for most businesses." He said he was sorry to hear that. "I am as well. Marsha has three kids she's trying to raise on a waitress's salary, and I don't think she's making it. Especially when she calls off so much."

"I waited on tables when I was in college once or twice. It was nice to be able to be around people when all I was doing was studying in my room. It got me out of the dorm sometimes, and I needed that." He finished off his burger and was glad that he had been brought another one to eat. "I've been working on contracts for the past three weeks, so this was quite a change for me to do. I really did have a good time."

"I hope you can say that tonight. Tonight will be twice as busy with it being Friday night all you can eat fish fry." He told Sammy that he was looking forward to it. "As I said, I hope you can say that at the end of the night. We're usually here until well past closing time just getting the place ready for Saturday lunch."

"I'm looking forward to it. Especially when I can spend some time with you, too. Maybe between tables we can say something about ourselves to keep us on our toes." She laughed just as he had hoped that she would. "You have a lovely laugh, and I enjoy hearing it from you. How long has it been since you really felt free enough to laugh at something?"

"Forever, it seems like. I've been so busy that I never took into account my own feelings. But I do want to succeed so that I'm not living out of a box anytime soon." He told her that they had enough money right now that they'd neither one would have to work again, and it wouldn't hurt them financially. "I'd still worry. I have worried about money my entire life. This restaurant was the only investment I made when I first started out being a billionaire. And since it makes me money enough to pay my bills and eat, I've held onto it even though I've been approached by buyers several times. I just find that I can't let go of it."

"I know what you're saying. I've held onto things that I should have sold off long ago, but for sentimental reasons, I hang onto them. I still have my first business, too, though it's not doing as well as this place seems to be. Do you work every day?" She said that she took off Monday and Tuesday so that she didn't burn herself out. "I can see that happening as well. I've been burnt out before when I thought that I needed to work to keep the place from going under."

"It's been fun here. I love this job. Even though no one here knows that I own this place, they have been respectful of my changes when I have to make them. The Friday night fish fry is a new thing, and it's made some really good money for this place. I don't know that I'd do it in another setting, but people seem to enjoy it a great deal and the staff makes a great deal of money on tips and such." He was enjoying his time talking to her and was sad when she started looking around as if she needed to get up and get going. "I have to make a deposit before tonight. I try to keep as little money in the place as I can on any one day."

"I don't blame you for that." When she got up and left him there to work, he cleaned up the table and reset it for tonight. The fish fry started at five o'clock, and it would be busy until they shut down at ten. He was going to need to go home and change, as Sammy told him he'd need to wear a tie tonight. Laughing to himself, he thought about the fact that he seldom wore a tie anymore since he'd been wearing jeans everywhere he went. Tonight was going to be a blast, he told himself.

At ten that night, he was ready to quit and go home. There were still tables to be bussed, and he had been having to pee since seven. Never did he work so hard in his life. But he had to admit, he did feel pretty good about what he'd been able to accomplish in such a short amount of time. Not only did he get all his tables cleaned off when they were needed, but he knew that some of his tables had turned four times tonight, thanks mostly to his being able to get them cleaned off and set up again.

"You have to take some of my money." He told Diana that he couldn't do that; he was being paid more than she was. "Well, you did me a solid tonight, and the rest of us, too, when you were so good at your job. I'm not going to be tipping James anymore. He's been a lazy fuck, and I saw it tonight. Did you know that he had to have a break in the middle of the rush when he was working? I doubt very much you've even had a drink of water since we started."

"I really did have fun. I'm worn out, I will admit that, but I really did enjoy myself tonight." She asked him what he was doing next Friday night, and they both laughed. "But seriously, I was just helping out when Sammy said you were shorthanded."

"And it doesn't hurt that she's beautiful too, does it?" He winked at her, and they both had another good laugh. "But thanks for tonight. I can now buy diapers and put gas in my car tonight. Woo hoo for me."

The rest of the night, while cleaning the last of the tables, he got more compliments from the staff. Even the cook said that he'd been almost too busy at one point when he needed a smoke. And now that he was stacking the plates right in the bus tub, he was even getting thanks from the dishwashers as well. The only person that he'd not heard from was Sammy, and she was locked in her office doing the nightly deposit along with paperwork.

After everyone had left, when the place was ready for tomorrow, he sat in the back room waiting for Sammy. She asked him to wait so that he could go with her to the bank, and he agreed. Usually, the cook went with her, but since he was there, he said he'd do it. It was going to be a nice deposit tonight, and he was happy for her.

Chapter 3

Allen knew that his daughters lived around here, but he didn't know how to find them. They'd been a pain in his ass since they'd been born, but now it was different. He'd had a change of heart about them doing anything for him. He wanted them to take care of him in his old age, and they were going to do it. At least he hoped so. He'd do anything to have them love him again. But it was a bit more than he thought he'd get from them, considering how he'd treated them as children. Convincing them that he was a changed man was going to be difficult for him and Belinda.

"Do you think we can make a few bucks by putting out a sign that says we're hungry, we'd get anything?" He said that he wasn't sure anymore about people. "I agree. They can be a bit mean to you when they think you ain't got two nickels to rub together."

They'd been looking in dumpsters for the last week, trying to get enough food to sustain them. It wasn't working out. First of all, it made him sick to his belly to even think about eating what they considered trash, and secondly, he was just too old to be getting in and out of dumpsters. It was a younger person's world of being homeless.

"Do you suppose if we found them, they'd buy us a meal or two?" He told Belinda that he doubted they'd hand over a free newspaper to them if they had one. "Yeah, I think you might be right on that. We weren't the best parents in the world. Though I think we were better than most."

"I'd say that's not true either. We were terrible people and worse to our children. Instead of treating them like the treasures that they are, we treated them less than some people do their own dogs. In fact, I think that dogs have a better life than we treated the girls." She didn't say anything, which he wasn't surprised. There were times when Belinda would lash out at him, and he expected no less of her today. However, she surprised him again by not saying anything.

They'd been terrible, is what they'd been. Starving them when they had food enough for all four of them. They'd even stuff themselves instead of sharing with their little girls. And locking them in the closet when they just couldn't stand their whining anymore. They had a good reason to whine, but it still didn't make them very tolerant of their needs.

"To be honest with you, Belinda, I'm doubting that they'd want a thing to do with us, and I can't say that I'd blame them. Not only were we terrible parents, we were just plain terrible people to everyone." He thought of the things that he'd said to his daughters when they were little. Hell, it didn't stop there; he'd said things to them that no parents should when they were teenagers, too. It hurt his heart every time he thought of the words that had come out of his mouth. "I'm not looking for them very hard, to be honest. I'm fearful of what they might say to me when we do catch up with them. And we'll deserve every word that comes out of their mouths, too. Especially Justine. She was the oldest, and we treated her poorly even before her sister was born. It wasn't their fault that they were born to us. We should have taken better care of them since they were ours."

"Then how do we tell them that?" He said that he didn't know, but had worked on it in his head. "They're not going to have a thing to do with us, and we both know it. We could be living the good life with them had we been nicer parents. But we weren't. I'm guessing that someday we're going to be found by a dumpster, dead, and no one will care. We just need to get with them for a few minutes. If they'd just let us talk to them and tell them how we feel now."

"It'll take a lifetime of apologies to get them to understand that we've changed." Belinda said she would be willing to try if they could find them. "As I said, I'm not looking all that hard for them, so I don't know what they'll say."

They continued to walk around the town. Allen was of the opinion that even if one of his girls were to walk right up to him and say 'hi,' he'd not know who they were. Almost nine years of being out of their life was a long time, and he knew that he was different looking, too.

"We're both older than we were when we went into the prison system. And we both know how hard that kind of life can be when you're locked up. Do you think that you'd know me when we were getting out if not for us talking when we could? Not neither one of them visited us, not that I blame them." Belinda said that she didn't blame them for that. They'd been mean. "We was mean and terrible people."

It took them nearly all day to find a place to hold up tonight. It was an old abandoned building along Main Street that had been falling into disrepair since before they went to prison. Now it was barely what they'd call a house; it was mostly in need of repair of the roof and walls now. But at least it had water that they could bathe in. That was a major plus for them.

They never took a bath if they didn't have to before prison. It wasn't until they couldn't stand themselves that they'd take a spit bath, a bath that only required the least amount of water and a rag to clean their most nastiest of places on them. Even then, they'd still smell, but not nearly as bad as before. The summers were the worst for them. Or other people around them, he supposed.

There were other habits that they used to do that they didn't anymore. And because they no longer drank pop or ate out all that much — not that they could afford that anymore — they had trimmed down quite a bit and were healthier for it. Walking around the town didn't bother them as much as it had before. And they didn't get winded anymore either. That was another reason that he wanted to get with his daughters so that they could eat better meals rather than getting their meals from the dumpsters. Just as he was getting ready to go into the building that they'd found, he saw his baby girl.

There was no mistaking her for anyone else. She still had her long hair that was plaited down the back in a neat braid. Her clothing was clean and neat-looking. But it was her eyes that made him know it was her. No one had those green eyes like she did, like shiny gems that she polished up every day before meeting the world. He continued to watch her as she made her way into the restaurant's front door. Unlocking and locking it back when she entered.

"Did you see something?" He told Belinda that he'd seen Sammy. "You should have told me. I would have loved to have seen her, too."

"She looks beautiful. And she must be the

manager of that store we like to go dumpster diving in. They have really nice food that comes out of there." Allen pointed to the place he'd seen her go in. "I'm wondering if we should wait for her to come out some night and try to talk to her. Can't hurt to try, can it?"

"If she don't pepper spray us first or pull out a gun." There was that, and he thought about what she'd been doing when she went into the place. "She might well talk to us, but she'd not trust us. Neither one of them should for all we did to them. I'm just sad we didn't change our ways before we went to prison, and we might have been able to talk to them some."

Belinda was right, as usual, about prison. They'd barely made it to their time getting out; they'd both been so depressed. If not for the prison helping them, they might not have come out in anything but a body bag; things were that difficult for them on the inside. Allen found himself watching the restaurant most of the night to see when she came out.

"Look, there she is." They both watched as she came out of the building and into an awaiting car. "I'm betting that they're headed to the bank to deposit the money. And that big fellow is her protection. Maybe we can get with him or something to talk. He might be able to get her to sit down with us for a little bit."

It wasn't going to happen. They didn't know who the man was; he'd never gotten out of the car, and it was too dark to see what color the vehicle was, too. Not to mention, they didn't know what sort of person he was, or even if he had any kind of relationship with Sammy that would want her to come and see them. It was all just too sad, he thought. It wasn't their fault, but he wished that he could get up the nerve to go and see her. Soon, the car came back, and she was dropped off by one of the cars in the lot. That was something that he could work with, he told himself. When she drove off, he made his way to his makeshift bed and laid down.

It was nice to have a roof over their head, even if it had more holes in it than his shirt did. Now, if he could only get in touch with his daughter, he could work things out with her and maybe have a meal or two with her. He promised himself that he didn't want much, just time to tell her how sorry he was.

Allen couldn't sleep. Thinking about how he'd been less than a block from one of his daughters made him anxious. He was fearful of what she might never want a thing to do with him, and that bothered him more than anything. He wasn't thinking she was going to just help them out, no, he knew better than to even think of that, but he did want— He rolled to his side to think about what he did want.

A place to stay would be nice, but he knew in his heart that they didn't deserve that. Maybe they did deserve it; they'd done their time, but perhaps it was too much to ask of her. Especially for all the times they'd hurt them and been cruel to them both. He did wonder what Justine was up to, and since he'd found out that Sammy was close, Justine would be as well. At least that's what he was hoping for. To be able to see both his girls would be a thrill for him. Just to see that they'd made a good life for themselves would be more than he could hope for.

"You're talking in your sleep again." He told Belinda that he wasn't asleep but mumbling about the hardness of the floor. "Well, maybe someone is throwing out an old mattress or one of them blow-up kinds, and we can get it out of the trash. That'd be nice, don't you think?"

He didn't want to sleep on anyone's tossed-out mattress, he started to tell her, but changed his mind. She was more than likely asleep already anyway. He thought about all the things that he thought that he'd like, and he kept coming back to his daughters and how they were doing right now.

Allen wanted a job where he could feel like a person again. He'd had one in prison, but it didn't pay all that much. However, it did give him a sense of being a man, something that he'd realized that he'd never felt until then. Their mode of having money back when they'd been raising the girls was when they could sucker some guy out of his wallet and take the cash. It was the way they did everything back then, take-take-take.

Wondering why he didn't tell Belinda what he'd been thinking gave him pause. There were times when he thought that she enjoyed being without anything to hold them down. That's what she'd said too, too many things would hold a person down, and he didn't believe that. He thought that while having a lot of useless things was terrible, not having anything to their name was worse.

He decided that he wanted a roof over his head that didn't leak and a soft bed. And some time with his daughters. He didn't think that was too much to want in this life. He figured that if he had money from a job, he could have food in his belly if he was smart enough to hold onto it. And Allen thought that he'd been so long without that he'd know the best way to hang onto a few dollars for some food. That was all he wanted. He didn't care about a television, lots of clothing, or even a nice chair that he could rest his bottom in. Just those three things would go a long way in making him feel like a man who had something to look forward to.

The sun was shining in the building when he realized that he'd not gotten one bit of sleep. Getting up when he heard the crunch of gravel, he watched as Sammy got out of the car she'd gotten in last night.

Then, when another car pulled up, he felt his eyes fill with tears when he realized that the other woman could have been Justine, but he just wasn't sure.

When they hugged one another, he looked harder at the two of them, just knowing that it was his daughters. There they were, standing not a fifty feet from him, and he couldn't do a damned thing about it. Watching them as they got back into Sammy's car, he had it in his head that they did this all the time. Meet here to go to lunch together someplace. Or in this case, breakfast. His belly rumbled in protest, but he didn't look away. This was a treat that he never expected and would cherish for the rest of his days. He'd gotten to see both his little girls, and they looked just great to him.

Lying next to Belinda, he let the tears fall. He thought that he should have awakened her, but there really wasn't time. Even to turn his back on the scene below him for a few seconds felt like he'd miss something wonderful. Now he had a moment in time that he'd look on as a gift he'd never thought he'd have, and he was somewhat glad that he'd not had to share it with Belinda. It was selfish, he knew, but he just couldn't count on her to see what he'd seen. He wanted it to be both his daughters there below him.

He decided that he was going to get their plate numbers so that he'd be able to see their cars when they were out and about. Just so he could catch a glimpse of them going about their daily routine like their father wasn't right there with them. Getting up when he realized that he wanted to know more about them and couldn't get it lying there, he made his way down the stairs to the parking lot and got Justine's license plate number. And when she returned, he'd get the same from Sammy's car.

~*~

Melbourne listened to the faerie as she told him where the Taylors were hiding. He remembered the look on Sammy's face when she thought that they were outside her door and knew that if she understood where they were right now, she'd be freaked out. Not to mention Justine, who he'd only met one time so far. They were both terrified of their parents, and with good reason, too.

He'd been able to read the report on their parents and how they'd been put in prison for child neglect as well as child endangerment. Justine had been an adult then and had been given custody of her younger sister. However, he couldn't see where she'd ever taken care of her little sister at all. She'd been so traumatized by their parents that it took her almost six years before she would leave the house that she grew up in. Terrified, he supposed of them coming back and taking up where they had left off.

His mom had been able to get him the paperwork from their time in prison. After the first year, they changed so dramatically that even the warden didn't believe their new personality. But they became model prisoners, never causing any trouble, and had gotten into a healthy program that had made them healthier than they'd been in their entire lives. Their one goal in life, they told the warden, was to be someone that their daughters could be proud of. Yet they never used their time in prison to contact either one of them, even though they might have had help from the system. Neither one of them wanted to bother their daughters for fear of what they still might think of them.

"I have a faerie on the two of them. The mister is a lot different than the missus. Not that she's outwardly mean, but I see some of her meanness coming out when she's frustrated about not having the things that she wishes for. She wishes for a good home with food in the cabinets as well as a car to get around in. The mister only wants a roof over his head as well as some time with his children. The missus never mentions the girls when she is upset." He asked Juice if either one of them had looked for a job. "The mister has looked, but since he has no address nor a working phone, he cannot get one. The misses has not. I don't know why, but I can find out for you."

"That's all right. Tell me what they've been

doing since they found a place they can sleep at night. I want to make sure that they're not plotting to harm the sisters." Juice told him that they seemed to be keeping up with walking as much distance as they can a day and getting themselves something to eat. "The building has water, doesn't it? I mean, I had you make sure that they could have at least that."

"They bathe daily, even though they complain about the water being very cold." That was good, he thought. At least they were trying. "Have you had any luck with talking to the man? I know you said that he watches Sammy nightly."

"I believe that he holds the place where his daughter works close to his heart. The misses doesn't seem to understand that he knows both their cars when he sees them. She seems to complain a great deal, but nothing ever comes from it. I believe that she simply likes to complain about things." It said that in the report from the prison. That Belinda was a nagger and complainer, but she never did anything to change the way that she could get to the things that she wanted. "Mr. Allen washes out their clothing nightly and hangs them up to dry. I have been making sure that they're stain-free and dry before morning. I hope that's all right."

"It is, and thank you." He thought of the other things that he had in mind for Allen. He seemed to be the one he could talk to. He'd not had any kind of contact with either of them, but he had a feeling that Belinda would demand things while Allen would be appreciative of anything that he got. "Contact me if he looks like he's going to approach either one of the women. He doesn't seem dangerous right now, but that doesn't mean that he's got a plot in his head that would harm them."

He knew that he didn't. All he wanted was to talk to the girls; he called them and maybe have a meal or two with them. While he didn't like eating from the dumpster, he would do it just knowing that he wasn't bothering his daughters about it. The man just wanted a relationship with his daughters, no matter how little it turned out to be.

After Juice left him to go and follow the Taylors around, he put everything that he had in a file. He knew he was being dishonest with Sammy about the information that he had, but he wasn't sure how she'd take them looking for them. Tonight, when he took her to the bank, he was going to have a talk with her about her dad and mom. That way, he could gauge how she wanted to proceed with whatever she wanted from them. Or them from her. Melbourne worried about Belinda some. She seemed to be unstable, but he wasn't sure that was all it was. She seemed to have two sides to herself, and neither one of them was anything that he'd trust as far as he could toss her. When Sammy touched his mind, he smiled. She was getting really good at doing something that she said she wouldn't do around him.

"I think I saw my parents today. At least my dad." He asked her where they were. "Out on Route Forty, just walking along the side of the road. It looked like they were collecting bottles or cans, but it was hard to tell."

"What if I told you that that's just what they were doing?" She asked him what he meant. "I have had a faerie on them since I found out where they're staying. It's not far from your place of work."

"Are they planning to harm me? If so, you'll have to visit me in jail because I'm no longer the little girl they abused." He said that as far as he could tell, her dad only wanted to talk to her, just to get to know her again. "Before they ram the knife in my back, you mean?"

"I don't think so." She didn't say anything for a long while, and he was worried that she was mad at him. "Your dad has been watching you come and go from the restaurant. I don't think he's told your mother that he knows where you are. I don't know that for sure, but that's just the feelings that I get from them. I've read both their minds, and neither one of them seems to have any kind of ill will toward either of you."

"Then what do they want?" He told her, as best he could, that her father wanted a job to feel like a human again, and her mother would just as soon have him pay for everything. "So she's no different than before." She paused, and before he could speak again, she did. "That was unfair. If he knows that I'm working here, he must know that I'm not worrying about what he can do to us. I'm supposing that they know where Justine is as well."

"Not that I've seen. They know both your cars, or at least he does. When he sees them out and about, whether in town or at the restaurant, he keeps an eye out for each of you. He acts like he's almost afraid to have you see him." She asked him if he knew what he wanted. "Nothing that I can sense. Like I said, he wants to talk to the two of you. Maybe have a meal with you, but nothing more than that."

"What about my mom? You don't mention her very much." He told her his opinion about her. "So she's just hanging onto dad for whatever he says. That's different for her. She was the one who would tell him to hurt us. I've always been more afraid of her than of him. She's the devil we used to call her."

"Since I didn't know them before, I can't judge them now. I know just what I've read in their minds." She again didn't say anything, and he was all right with that. Then she did ask him how long he'd been watching them. "About a week now. At least since you and I worked together that Friday evening, I saw him again when I took you to the bank that night. He was hanging around the vacant building across from your place. I've since found out that they're staying there. It has no heat, but it does have running water for them to use."

"Right now, I don't know what to do about them. I guess they're all right where they are." He said that he could have them moved out by the police. "No, don't do that. Just let them stay there until I can figure out what they're doing. I don't believe for a minute that they're just hanging around us waiting for a chance to talk. There has to be more to this than that."

"I'll do whatever you want. You just say the word and I'll have them out of that place by the end of the day." She again told him to wait, and he was all right with that. "However, if they try to hurt you, there will be no place they can hide that I don't find them. Understand?"

"I do, and I think I love you for that." His heart swelled in his chest at her words. Since he already loved her and she thought that she loved him, it was making him feel things that he'd never felt before. He felt like a new man and all because of her. "Look, I need to get some work done. I'll see you after work tonight, and I'll think about everything you told me. Is there anything else I should know about them?"

"Not them, but I'd not mentioned anything to your sister. I saw her in town yesterday, and she seemed stressed out. Again, I don't know her all that well from before she knew they were hanging around, but she seems like she's one short scare from being locked up. Is that normal for her?" Sammy told him that she was usually stressed out all the time, but she had been more so lately. "I can understand that. You guys went through hell and back with them from what I've found about their trial."

For the rest of the afternoon into the evening, he tried to get some work done. It wasn't easy; his mind kept going to his mate and her family, but he did manage to get two of the contracts read over from the city and one list of things that he wanted to talk to his mom and dad about.

His dad was an ancient and powerful vampire when he met their mom. Mom was older than Dad by a great many years, so together their magic was powerful. And in turn, they'd passed down their magic to their six sons, who in turn shared it with their mates when they came along. They had powerful magic as well, which usually didn't have anything to do with their mates. Like Amy could jump from flame to flame, looking as if her body was completely engulfed in the flames to get from one point to the other, Dad likened her magic to one very old, even older than him, and a powerful vampire; she was so strong.

None of the other mates were as strong as Amy, nor were any of the brothers as strong as her mate, his brother Fowler. They were to be king and queen of the faeries and other worldly creatures someday, and he would need to be strong in order to be able to do the job that had been in his family since the beginning of time. His mom and dad were taking care of the magic these days while their grandma saw the world that she helped to create.

After getting as much done as he could, Melbourne went to the website that listed homes for sale. There were plenty of them in his price range, but he knew that they were going to need something bigger than the condo that they both owned. He didn't know what Sammy was going to do with hers, as she owned the entire subdivision where she lived, but he was going to put his on the market as soon as they found a house they could both live in.

After finding several that he liked, he called the realtor that all of the family had been using and asked her to set up some times on Saturday morning to see the ones he'd asked about. Two of them he was ready to write off but there were three that he thought would be perfect for the two of them. He'd pick up Sammy and they'd see the houses before she had to work that evening. Melbourne was about as excited as he'd been in some time.

Going to see his parents, always a treat for him, he handed his dad the list when he told him why he was there. Dad said he could answer most of them as he'd heard the questions before from his brothers, but not all of them. He would have to see his mom or grandma to see if she could get him the information that he might need.

"I didn't know that Grandma was home. I thought that she was at an amusement park having fun." Dad told him that she'd gotten bored with that after the first day. "It really isn't as much fun to see one of those parks alone. It's always better to take someone with you."

"We told her that, but she said that she didn't know who she'd bring with her. I told her that I'd go with her and have a day of it, but she wouldn't hear of taking me away from work. I think this job is too easy for your mother. I look for her every day to say she can't stand the boredom anymore. Your grandmother ran such a tight ship here that the place practically runs itself. I myself enjoy all the creatures around and have the best time when it's time to open up the faerie blooms."

"I've seen that once. It is a beautiful time of the year. To see all the new faeries born out of the blooms is the most exciting thing I've ever witnessed. And when they have to test their wings, it's just too beautiful to describe in mere words." Dad agreed with him. "I might have to bring Sammy here when that's happening again. I'm sure that she'll enjoy it."

After Dad answered his questions, he went to find Grandma. He was thinking that he'd take her to the park with Sammy and they'd make a day of it. She'd enjoy spending time with him, and he'd love just watching Sammy and Grandma get to know one another.

Chapter 4

Now that she knew he was looking for her, Sammy watched out for her dad. Sometimes she'd see him with Mom, but most of the time he would be alone. She didn't approach him, but she did keep an eye out for him when she was out doing things. Most of the time, she would pretend not to see him, but after a while, it got to be too much for her, and she'd make sure that when she did see him, she'd go into another shop just so he couldn't get to her.

It's not that she didn't believe Melbourne when he told her what her dad's intentions were; she was just cautious about him coming around her. She remembered the beatings that she had taken as a child, and her mind made up all kinds of excuses not to be around him. She was tempted to just walk right up to him and ask him what he wanted. Nearly bumping into him on the main street, she did just that.

"I just want to talk to you." She asked him about what, she had her life just the way that she wanted it. "I'm sure you do. You always were one to get what you wanted when you saw it. I swear I don't want to hurt you again. I think that I did enough of that when you were a child. And you can't imagine how terrible I feel about that."

"Then why did you do it?" He seemed startled by the question, so she asked him something else. "Why did you have us if you only wanted to starve us most of the time or beat us. I think I asked you that once when I was a child, and you never answered me."

"No, I wouldn't have back then. I would have just back-handed you and been done with your questions. But I want you to know that I'm a different man than I was back then. And I wanted to tell you and your sister how sorry I am for the man and father that I was. You've no idea how many sleepless nights I've had just thinking about talking to the two of you. Is Justine all right? Is she getting her life together, too?"

"She's fine when she thinks that you two were in prison. Right now, she's very stressed out, thinking that you're going to come back and start on us again. I have no reason to believe that you won't, so I don't know what to tell her." She saw the tears well in his eyes and felt bad about them. She'd caused them by being cruel, and she didn't like that of herself. "I'm sorry. I had no right to talk to you like that. Even though I think you might be all right around me, I just don't know anymore. Do you need a job?"

"It's difficult to find one with my background. People take one look at the prison term and send me on my way. I heard that the place where you work hires ex-cons, but no one who has abused their partner or children. I'm certain I know the reason why you don't want them around you. We were never good at being parents."

"No you weren't." She thought about what she was doing and decided to take a chance. "Would you like to have lunch with me? I don't know where Mom is right now, but I'd like to take you to lunch. We can talk then."

"I'd like that. I surely would." She pointed to the deli/hamburger place close to where they were standing, and they went there. There were plenty of people around that she didn't have to worry about him hurting her, and it was an open space so that she could get away if he had other things in mind while eating with her. After they both ordered, she told him that they'd get something for her mom for him to take back with him. "She'd like that, I'm sure."

He hesitated, and she wondered what that was about and asked him. He gave her an excuse that she might be upset because she couldn't talk to her as well. Just as she was going to say then forget it he smiled brightly at her and said he'd enjoy just the two of them having a meal. In fact, he'd been thinking about her a great deal.

Once they ordered, the two of them scoped out

a picnic table for them to use. Since they had a number that they picked up their food with, the two of them sat down under the biggest tree she'd ever seen. The cool breeze felt good coming from the shade, and she put her face up to catch a few rays. Her dad told her that she was beautiful. Without looking at him, she frowned.

"You've never said that to me before." She looked at him then. "In fact, I don't believe I've ever heard you say that you loved me either. Not that it matters now, I suppose, but that just occurred to me."

"I'm sorry. I truly am. I suppose telling you now that I love you is a little too late." She said she didn't know if she believed him or not. "Fair enough. I never deserved your love or your respect. I still don't. But I'd like the chance to earn that right again."

"We'll see. I'm not trying to be cruel or anything, but I don't know this new you, and it's difficult to trust you right now." Again, he said that he understood. "I'm not going to bring up the past right now. What did you want to talk to me about?"

"The past. I'm sorry for the way that I treated you. And if you were to walk away right now, it's no more than I deserve for the way that I treated you and your sister. While I understand that, my heart would like to make amends to you. Given the chance, I'd like to be able to try very hard to earn your love and trust."

She asked him what Mom wanted to do. "I don't know, to be honest with you. And I plan on doing that from now on, to be honest with you and Justine."

"What does she say?" She thought about it and shook her head. "It doesn't matter. I'll give her whatever I can until she hurts me again. Then there will not be any second chances with me. I'll close that door so fast that you'll never be able to get to me again. Neither of you."

"Is that what this is? A second chance for me?" She told him it was until he messed up again. "You believe that I will. That I'll mess up like I did before and hurt you. I won't. I'm working on trying to regain a relationship with you, and if you continue to act like you are now, then yes, I'll give you whatever you need. Within reason. You've had a long time to think about what you wanted to do, and I've only had the last hour."

"Yes, I have. And again, I'm sorry about that." He looked up when they called their number and went to get their lunch. She made sure she knew where all the places were that she could hide if he were to get violent with her again. When he returned, he set the sub aside for Mom and opened the waxed paper around his. "Your mother will be so jealous. Not for the food, though, that will please her a great deal, but that I'm getting to have a nice lunch with you. Tell me about yourself. I want to know it all."

She started with Melbourne. "He's my mate. I'm assuming you know what that is?" He said that he did and congratulated her on finding him. "He says that I found him, but I don't know what the difference is. He'd be here now, but I didn't tell him I was meeting with you. He's very protective, I've noticed."

Sammy didn't tell him about the lottery that she'd won, nor the fact that she owned the restaurant where she worked. These were things that she wasn't ready to share just yet. Instead, she told him about her adulthood from the time they were in prison, not keeping anything back about how she'd struggled hard to make sure that she had a roof over her head and money enough for emergencies in the bank. By the time they'd finished their meal, she was exhausted. She'd been so tense since she'd first spoken to him that she'd worn herself out just stressing about whether or not he'd hurt her. When she looked around again, she noticed that Melbourne was at another table having lunch with two of his brothers, and she could have kissed him. He was there in case things went south, yet far enough away that he wasn't crowding her while she had a long conversation with her father. She was going to have to figure out a way to thank him for his kindness today.

When he looked her way, she waved him

over to meet her dad. After introducing the two of them, Melbourne sat down but didn't take over the conversation. Instead, he waited for her to include him in whatever they were talking about. Melbourne was a good man, and she thought perhaps she'd missed that when she'd first met him.

It was then that she realized that the man she was falling in love with knew more about her than her own father did, and that saddened her. Just as Melbourne was getting up to leave, he had a lot of work to do, he told her. He took her father's hand into his much larger one before speaking.

"You hurt her or Justine, I'll kill you." Dad nodded, and she could see the tears again. Then he told her mate that he would allow him to kill him if he did. "Just so we're clear on that, then I can go away now. If you're still looking for a job, I have one for you. It's not a shit job, but it's not the greatest either. I will pay you a good wage and expect a good work effort from you. If you'd like to take me up on that, just call my office. If you don't have the means to call, then stop by. It's the building on Main Street called Welsh, Inc."

"Are you giving me this job because you want to keep an eye on me? If so, thank you. I want to be a better man and father than I was, and having a job will help me with that." Melbourne nodded and said he was going to keep an eye on him. "I'll do what it takes to get myself up and on my feet. I don't have anything but the clothing on my back, but they're clean and so am I."

"I'll speak to you when you come by." Then he left them there. Going to where his brothers were, Melbourne winked at her before leaving the area and going back to work. She looked at her dad and wondered what he saw when he saw the big man. A threat or a nice person because as surely as she was sitting here, she knew him to be both.

"He's a good man." She said she was just thinking about that. "He loves you, too. You can see it in the way that he looks at you when he thinks that no one is watching."

"I've never been loved before. I think I could get used to it." Dad laughed, like he'd forgotten that he could do something like that, and it made her laugh all the harder for it. "You should laugh more often. Then it won't startle you so much when you do. It's a nice sound too. I don't think I've ever heard you laugh before."

"I had no reason to laugh before, but today is a beautiful day and I'm having lunch with my equally beautiful daughter. Life has suddenly taken a good turn, and I'm not even going to wait for the other shoe to drop. This is the best day of my life." He laughed a bit more before he looked at her with a huge grin on his face. "Thank you for today. If I never get to have another lunch with you, then I will treasure this time for all of eternity. You're a beautiful woman with a big heart, and I can't thank you enough for sharing it with me today. But I've taken up enough of your time for one day, and I need to get this to your mother. Would you like to have lunch with her sometime? I can tell her when you're not busy."

"I'd like that." Really, if she were honest with herself, which she rarely wasn't, she didn't want to have lunch with her mother. From the little hints that her dad had given her, she wasn't going to be as nice as he'd been today. She didn't know why she believed that, but she did. "The next time I see you, I'll have a cell phone for you so that you can contact me when you want to meet again."

"That would be lovely. I'll take good care of it. I can use it for work too when Melbourne calls me for a job. I can't wait to begin working. I feel lazy not having anything to do when I'm just wandering around." She told him that she'd have it tomorrow so that he could contact her with the times he could have lunch, and she stood up to leave. "This really has been the best day of my life, Sammy. Thank you for talking with me and eating a meal with me."

"You're welcome." She made her way to the restaurant and let herself inside. Standing with her back to the door, she stood there for several minutes just breathing in and out. She hoped that she wasn't just played for a fool. She had enjoyed herself and wanted to do it again. Not tomorrow, but soon. For as much as she wanted to have a meal with her father again, she didn't want to have one with her mother.

~*~

Belinda didn't like that Allen had gotten a job before she'd been able to. She wanted to be first in that, but she supposed it was all right. One of them needed to work, and it might as well have been him. But the sub he'd brought her home kind of pissed her off. Why didn't he insist that she be there with their daughter, too? She was trying to make amends, too, wasn't she?

He had told her what they had talked about. And that her mate had threatened him. She was pissed off about that, but he seemed to think it was the right thing to do. She would have been all over the man for saying that he'd kill him, but Allen said that he would allow him to kill him if he were to hurt her.

"What if you accidentally hurt her somehow? Am I going to be left out in the cold without you around? That seems like a terrible threat that someone could give a person." He told her that she knew what he meant but was being silly about it. "I'm not being silly about anything. You know how much I hate it when you call me that. I'm being serious right now. He could kill you, and I'd be all alone. Since I didn't get to have a nice lunch with our daughter."

"I told you it was just something that happened. She was coming down the sidewalk, and there was no time for me to hide." She asked him why he'd have to hide if it were their daughter. "I didn't want her to think that I'd been stalking her. And I wasn't, not really. I was just seeing her around town for the last several days, and I enjoyed that."

"So you have been stalking her. Maybe I would have been with you had you told me what you were doing." He said that he'd not done anything, but she had invited him. "I wonder if she would have invited us both had we been together."

"Why are you being like this? I told you that she wanted to have lunch with you sometime, didn't I?" She said that it sounded last-minute to her. "How would you even know if it was last-minute or not. You weren't there."

"I know this." Her lunch was ruined because they were fighting, and she told him that. Once she wrapped her sandwich back up and put it near her other things, she told him she needed to go out. "I might just run into her, too. Where did you say that she worked?"

"I don't know." She knew he was lying, but rather than get into a big fight with him again, she was just going to let him stew about her being mad at him. And she was too. They were partners in this, and he was getting out of line. It took her ten minutes of stomping around to realize that it was much too hot out for her to be out in the sunshine and that she didn't even know what her daughter might look like. Either one of them, for that matter. "I just bet that he does."

She started talking to herself when she was in prison. It was the best way to get someone to agree with her, and she liked it when people stayed away from her, thinking that she was off her noodle. It also afforded her someone to talk to in the middle of the night when she couldn't sleep. People might think that she was insane, but she knew better. She just liked her own company.

Sitting on one of the pretty benches that were along the main street of the little town, she looked around. The place had changed a great deal since she'd been living around here. There were more shops than there had been before, and she liked to go into them to see what sort of pretties they had. Of course, she did take a few things when she was in the ones that seemed to cater to her needs, but not too much so that she'd end up in prison again.

She was almost sure that the woman who owned the shop had been keeping an eye out for her. Every time she went into the store, she followed her around like she was just waiting for her to take something. She wasn't stupid enough to think that she'd be able to get off with a stern warning, but was careful that she didn't get caught. Belinda never wanted to go into the system again. It had been too hard on her, and she'd never forgive her daughters for saying all those things about her when there had been a trial. But she was going to make nice for some things that she needed. A house for one thing. A pretty one with a picket fence in the front yard and a big porch that wrapped around the house so that she could spy on her neighbors. It was harmless, she thought, and something that she missed when she'd been locked up.

She also wanted some money. And to never have to eat from a dumpster again. It was worse than jail food, and she'd never thought that she'd say that. Stomping her foot, she thought of Allen again talking to Sammy without her around. He did it on purpose, she just knew it.

Belinda would have done things differently when she'd found her daughter. She would have demanded money...in a nice way. Then asked for someplace to sleep that wasn't an empty building that leaked when it rained and had cold water all the time, what she wouldn't give for a nice hot bath with lots of bubbles.

While still sitting on the bench, she looked

around at all the people who were walking around. Like they didn't have a care in the world, she thought meanly to herself. Shaking her head at herself, she thought that if she had to go one more day with her husband talking about how they were changed people, she'd puke. She was changed, but it wouldn't take her very long to be knocking the shit out of someone that pissed her off.

Being thinner helped her with her health, too. When she'd been overweight, she'd had trouble going up and down stairs in prison. But once she started having to take them to get around, she noticed that the pounds just shed away like it had been a hot day with a chocolate bar in her pocket. She pulled out the bar of candy that she'd swiped last night and decided it was the perfect time to get her fill of the sweet treat. She could never pull it out and eat it in front of Allen.

He'd have a fit about it and would tell her that she was going to end up back in prison if she were to keep it up. It was just one little candy bar, not like she was robbing the place of all its cash. For as much as she was tempted to do that, she knew that to be caught would take her right back to the place she'd only just been released from, and she didn't want that.

His keeping her on a tight leash bothered her, too. He was forever telling her to behave herself in the event that she got caught. What were they going to do with an aging old woman who liked to get her thrills out of stealing from merchants that seemed to have too much anyway? Put her in jail? For a fifty-cent candy bar? A three-dollar tube of lotion. She pulled it out and used some of it on her hands. She'd never had such pretty-smelling stuff before that belonged only to her.

Belinda knew that she could get used to the finer things in life. She'd never had her nails done until she was in prison, and one of the other women would do them for a price. She loved having her hair washed by someone else, too, just to get all the tightness out of her head until she was nothing more than a limp noodle. There were plenty of things that she missed about prison, but the solitude. She couldn't stand her own company for very long, and she knew it. All the talking to herself aside, if she had to be by herself for long periods of time, she'd lash out at someone and get herself into trouble again. It was the way it had been going on since she'd been a child.

She didn't know how long she sat there, but the sun was starting to go down. Getting up and making sure that she didn't have any evidence of the chocolate or the lotion on her person, she made her way back to the building where they were staying. She did wonder why no one had run them off and thought that the security around here was very lax. Another reason why she didn't think they'd bother with her stealing was that they had other important things to do before getting to her and her petty theft. She might even get herself some of the pretty bottles of lip gloss the next time she was in one of the little shops.

When she was where they were sleeping, Allen was gone again. Not that she really cared, but he'd been leaving her alone a great deal over the last several days. She was going to have to talk to him about it. When he got a job, she would need something to do, or she could go with him. Whatever the work that he was going to be doing was, surely they'd not care if she were to hang around for a bit now and then.

It was coming on dark when he returned home. She'd eaten the sub and thought that it was delicious. She'd not tell him, of course, nor would she thank Sammy for it when it was her turn to have lunch with her. And she most certainly wouldn't be bringing back a sub for Allen. She wanted to dine in a restaurant, like the one across the street from where they were squatting.

Looking out the window that looked right into the parking lot, she wondered what sort of food they'd have in such a place. People were usually dressed up when they went inside the place, and she noticed that a great many people brought some of the food out with them in bags. She'd never do that. If she couldn't eat it all at one sitting, then she'd leave it to prove that she had money to burn. Maybe she'd have Sammy or Justine take her there when it was her turn. They were probably taking turns with feeding them because it was costing so much for one. But then she remembered that he'd brought her food too and wondered again why she'd not been invited when her father had been there. Belinda wondered if he even thought of her when he was eating with their daughter.

"Justine. I need to find her." Why she thought that Justine would be any different than Sammy was about taking them out to lunch, but she remembered that when she was younger, she would be the one who cracked first. She'd be sobbing even before they hit her, and she never understood that when they were little. She also had the most fun with Justine when she'd been trying to protect her sister. That only happened once or twice before Sammy would protect Justine. And she was meaner than her older sister, too, by a great deal.

"What are you going on about? And why do you smell like candy?" She told him that she'd swiped a candy bar at the store, and he acted like she'd robbed the place of all its cash. "It will get you put back in prison, Belinda. What will you do then? I'm not going to be hanging around you anymore if you think that stealing is the way to go. Good lord, are you trying not to get with our daughters anymore? One screw up and they'll toss us aside like yesterday's old newspaper.

Don't do that again, all right?"

"I was hungry for something that didn't come out of a dumpster if you want to know the truth. And it was only about fifty cents. No one is going to take me back to prison for one half a dollar of a candy bar. They have better things to do, I would imagine." He said that once he had a paycheck, then he'd buy her candy bars. "To be honest with you, Allen dear, it sort of made me sick."

She needed him not to understand that she wasn't as good as he was. He might be driving her crazy with his rules about getting caught and seeing their daughter, but they were rules that were going to get them what they needed. Some money and a home. Surely their daughters would want to see them with the finer things of life after all this time?

"I talked to that man about a job. He's going to have me start in the morning. I'll be gone from eight until five or so. So you'll need to get your own lunches and dinner for a while. Just until I get us a check and we can use the money to get us some food from a real place." She asked him if she could come with him as she'd be bored all day. "No, you can't come with me. Do you want me to lose the first chance we've had since getting out of prison? You can find something to do around the town. Go to the library and read a book. I know they won't let you check one out without a form of identification, but you can sit in there and read a book or a magazine if you behave."

Belinda wanted to snarl at him that behaving wasn't getting her anywhere, but eating out of dumpsters, but she was trying to be on her best behavior right now. And she might not be able to have lunch with Sammy and Justine if she were to be bad. She was tired of the rules that got her nothing but a headache. Biting her tongue, she watched as he rinsed out his clothing for tomorrow and then took a freezing shower. Christ, but this was getting harder each day to be like Allen so she could have her time with the girls. And she was going to have it by god if it was the last thing she did in this life.

Lying down on the hard floor when Allen did it took her forever to get comfortable enough to try and sleep. Once she rolled to her back, she was glad that the weather had turned hot so that she could sleep without a blanket. She wanted a pillow and was tempted to get up and get Allen's shirt to use, but it would be too much effort. Besides, he really needed to work so that they could start having things that they needed. Money was the first thing that popped into her head, and she couldn't wait to see what sort of things she could do with a bit of cash now and again.

She just hoped that she could convince her daughters that she was as good as gold so that they'd set her up in a house. She didn't care if Allen wanted to live with her, too; she just wanted a place to live so that she could have something of her own around her. Even if she had to steal them to get them, as she kept telling herself, no one was going to bother with an old woman who stole things that she needed. They might even have a pity party for her and one of those GoFundMe things where someone put a sad story online and then they gave them money. She could use one of those things about now.

Chapter 5

Melbourne had made up a job for Allen just so he could keep an eye on him during the day. If he could have had him working later in the evening, he would have done that too, but right now, he was working out better than he thought that he would.

The job was simple enough. He was to walk up and down each street and tell him if the house was empty or not. Then, if it was, had anyone put a sign in the yard to tell if there was a realtor involved. He did need the information, but he could have done it himself. This way, Allen wasn't stuck in the house all day with Belinda, and he thought that the man was enjoying himself.

Yesterday, Sammy had gotten him a cell phone, and he thought that the man was going to cry; he'd been so happy about it. After showing him how to program the numbers in of himself and Sammy, he put it in his pocket but kept checking to make sure it was there. When he went into prison, cell phones hadn't been as big a deal as they were now, and he wondered if he'd ever had one. Thinking that he'd not, he decided to make sure that he knew how to answer it, too, if someone called him.

Today, Sammy was bringing by her sister to talk to their father, and he was worried about how that would go. Justine was just too stressed for her to find any enjoyment in meeting up with her father, and he worried about her health. But Sammy knew her sister better than he did, so he tried his best not to be involved in what she had going on. At a quarter to noon, both women showed up, and he was glad that he'd had Allen pick up lunch on his way into the office today. It would be a good meeting, he hoped, and he'd be there if things got out of hand.

He met the other man at the door when he saw him walking toward the building. He warned him that both his daughters were there, and he stood stiff as a board without saying a word to him. The look on his face was very telling.

"It's all right, Allen. We're all going to have lunch together and have some fun." He just stared at him. "I'll be right here if anything goes wrong."

"Don't kill me if it doesn't. I want to talk to them both, so if you could not kill me when something happens, I'd appreciate that." Melbourne said that he wasn't going to kill him over a stressful meeting. "I hope not. I'm about as stressed out as I've ever been in my life. Just...I don't know, will you help me get through this?"

"I promise that I will. Just be yourself and you'll be fine." He was beginning to really like the other man and was glad that he was working for him. Now, if he could get Belinda a job too, then he thought that they'd be well on their way to making something of their life. He was still working on what she could do today. Allen said she'd take just about anything that he offered her, but he wasn't so sure. He'd caught some glimpses of the real Belinda just this morning when he'd seen her out and about alone. The four of them sat at the conference table just outside his office, and he began handing out the food. "I hope you don't mind, but I got French fries as well. They were having a special on combos, so I got us all one."

"I love French fries. Especially the shoestring style that they have there." He could have kissed Sammy for her trying to make everyone relax. "I've been looking forward to this all day. Haven't you, Justine?"

"I don't know." She glanced at her father, then away to her sister. "Are you sure he's not going to hurt me? They always acted like they were nice until we were alone with them. Are you sure I'm going to be all right?"

"You're going to be fine, I promise." She looked at him, and he smiled. "Dad, why don't you tell us about your job. Melbourne said that you've been doing a good job by finding the empty buildings that might need to come down."

"I've been walking the streets with a little map and marking the houses that have been left abandoned. Like the one that we're living in right now. It has running water, so it's not so bad, but in the winter months, it's going to be difficult to stay warm. I'm hoping that I can save up enough money to rent one of them." Allen handed the ketchup to Justine, and she nearly jumped up when he accidentally touched her fingers. He looked at Melbourne. "She's just nervous that I'm going to hurt her. I don't blame her much; I've been a terrible father to them both."

"You really were, and I don't understand how you think I'm just going to be all right with you doing it again." He told Justine that he'd never harm her at all. Never again. "I've heard about people saying that, but it's been too long since you've been around. What made you change into someone nice?"

"That's a fair question. I talked to a priest while I was in prison, and he told me that I couldn't be a better man unless I lived in your shoes for a while. I didn't know what he meant, and I didn't take him all that seriously at first, but after a while, he wore me down into thinking and knowing that what I'd done to you two was the worst kind of thing to have done."

"You really did. And I'm not going to just jump

right back to where we were either. You were cruel and hateful to us both. It took me a long time to be able to be by myself without jumping out of my skin every time someone came too close to me." He said he was sorry. "That doesn't cut it. I'm sorry, but you're going to have to do something more than just say that you're sorry. You're going to have to prove that you've become a changed man." She stood up. "I'm sorry. I'm not ready for this right now." Allen stood up as well and put up both his hands when she backed away from him.

"I just need a chance, Justine. A chance to prove to you both that I'm not the same person that I was before. And I'll do whatever it takes to make you believe me. Just tell me what it is you want from me." She said that she didn't know. "I can understand that. I do. I'll just keep trying until you're ready to forgive. If not forgive me, then at least give me a second chance in this life."

"I'll try." She sat back down and stared at her dad. "I don't know what to do with all these feelings and emotions that you've brought up by being this close to me. I've been dealing with this since I was a child, and I can't just turn it off. You've had a long time to forgive yourself, but I've not."

"I'm going to do my best to make sure you feel safe around me. I'm going to tell you every day that I love you, too. And that I'll beg for your forgiveness from now on." She didn't say anything, and Melbourne thought that was very telling for her. "I'm sorrier than I've ever been about what happened between us. You've no idea how angry I get at myself for not being a good father. Or at least one you could trust not to harm you when you're around me."

"I'll work on it on my end as well. Just don't expect me to be able to just jump right in and be the daughter I could have been. You were never nice to us. You were a terrible father. I can tell that you're working on this, but I'm going to need time." He told her to take as much time as she needed, and he'd be there for her. Melbourne could tell that she was trying to believe him, but it had been just too many years with him being the man that he'd been before prison. "I just need time. If you could give me that, I'll work on trusting you not to hurt me. Not just physically but mentally too."

"I understand." Allen wiped at the tears that were streaming down his cheeks. "I promise you that I'll be a good father and better man than I was. I won't do you any harm at all. On that, you have my word."

The rest of lunch was everyone talking. He could tell that Justine was making an effort to include her father in her conversations, but she was slightly stiff and sometimes had to take several deep breaths before she spoke to him. All in all, Melbourne thought it was a good first time for them getting together, and he couldn't wait to see it when they got to the point where they were all getting along. It was Sammy who talked about their mother.

"I honestly don't know what sort of person she's going to be." Justine asked their dad what he meant. "She's still bitter about being put into prison. I don't know that she's going to be able to sit with us without losing her temper. As you might remember, it's quite a temper she had on her."

"She'll either be nice or she'll be cut off from seeing us. We will fight back now, we're adults and know how to protect ourselves." Their dad only nodded and said they'd see. "You think she'll want to hurt us again? You know physical hurts aren't as bad as verbal ones. And I won't put up with mental hurts either. She can just go fuck herself if that's the way she's going to be."

Allen said that he didn't know what was in her mind, but Melbourne did. He didn't need a connection to her to be able to read her mind, and at this moment, all she was thinking about was how to get a nice home from her children, as well as money enough that she wouldn't have to do without. Even as they all sat there, Belinda was thinking that she'd bully Justine into what she wanted, as she wasn't as strong as Sammy. He didn't think that that would bode well for her, Belinda or not.

She was going to be in for a rude awakening if she thought that either Sammy or himself would allow her to bully the older sister. She was his family now, and he'd do everything within his power to make sure that she was safe from her. His entire family would.

After lunch, things were cleaned up, and Justine had left for her job, the three of them sat around and talked about anything other than Belinda. Even Allen went out of his way not to talk about his wife, and he thought that he might be right in his thinking that she wasn't going to be able to be around the girls. He finally asked if he thought that she'd be all right with him seeing the two of them or not.

"I don't care. Like Justine said, we're all adults now, and if she wants to cause trouble, I want nothing to do with it." Sammy asked if he thought that she would cause trouble. "I don't know. I don't believe that she'll try to cause hurt to the two of you, but I just don't know. While we were behind bars, she talked about how she really wanted to get a new house and money all the time, but she never had a plan to make it happen. She doesn't care for the fact that I'm working all the time. She'd rather I be there for her when she wants to talk to me. To be honest, I never told her about the cell phone that you gave me for work and to get in touch with you. I won't either if I can help it. I don't want her bothering my two girls for things that she should be working for."

He loved that Allen was being honest about his relationship with his wife. And he was glad too that he didn't mind telling Sammy that if she caused trouble or said anything other than what he said to her, then he was going to leave her. He was trying his best to make amends, and he didn't want Belinda to cause him heartache when he was working so hard at making it work.

Melbourne was going to send a faerie to keep an eye on Belinda. If she caused them any trouble, he wanted a heads-up about it before she did anything to jeopardize the relationship that was slowly building between Allen and his two children. He was also going to have a talk with Sammy about what he'd already found out about her. There was no way that he was going to allow them to be blindsided by anything that she said or did.

It was nearly quitting time for him when Allen came back to the office. He'd been showing up right before he left for the last three days. Just to tell him what he'd been able to figure out with the houses. Melbourne had been surprised at the number of houses that were ready to be torn down and the empty ones that were up and down just Main Street. He was going to have his family get right on some of the ones that could be saved. The rest that needed to be torn down would leave room for other houses to go in and make the street look so much better.

"You're doing a great job, Allen. I didn't realize that there were that many homes on the main drag that needed attention. And the fact that you found out that people are using them too was a surprise. I noticed, too, that you included the house that you and Belinda are living in." He said that he thought it needed a new roof, but the structure of the building was in fine shape. "You also said you have running water. I wonder how that works in the colder months."

"I've not been there yet, but most of the roof is gone, and we pretty much sleep under the stars every night." He laughed. "Belinda sleeps right through it all, but if there's a thunderstorm, I'm trying to find a place for me to keep dry. She'll just never wake up."

"That's some hard sleeping." He said that she'd always been one to sleep like that when he'd be up several times in the night to move around some. "I usually sleep well when I'm in a bed that fits my size. I'm six foot ten inches and need a specially sized mattress when I get into bed."

"I bet you do." He wasn't saying much, but Melbourne could tell that he had something on his mind. Or at least he thought that he did. He didn't know the man well enough yet to get his emotions down yet, but he was working on it. Then he finally asked. "I would like someplace to live. Do you think that you could help me?"

"I will if you want. However, as I've said to you before, I won't tolerate you hurting my mate or her sister." He nodded and said that he understood. "What kind of place are you looking to get into? Nothing large, I'm assuming."

"No, nothing like that. In fact, I wouldn't mind just a room in this building. I noticed that there is a bath and a kitchen here that I could use. Belinda, too, if she's willing." He asked him if he thought Belinda was going to be trouble. "Yes. Yes, I do. I don't know what kind of trouble she'll cause, but I fully expect her to make a stink out of something that isn't being done for her. Since I've been working, I've noticed how bitter she is about everything. I've never told her who I'm working for, nor the fact that you're Sammy's mate. I think she'll be hitting you up for things, too. I don't know that for sure, but I have it in my head that she's going to be nasty to the girls when they don't come through on what she wants."

"What is it you think she'll want?" Allen looked around like he was fearful that she might be close enough to hear him. "Allen, I need to know if you think she's going to cause trouble for the women. My family will protect you, too, if you tell me you want that. But I can't help you if I don't know what's going on."

"She's going to expect things to go back to the way they were before we went to prison. She'll want a large house, bigger than anything you and Sammy will have. She'll expect to be pampered, too." Allen's face went a little pink. "She'll hate that I want to live in this building with you working here too. It will be less than perfect for her, and I've only just come to realize that things have to be her way or no way. Even when you've paid me some extra money, I find myself not telling her about it. As I said, I don't know what she'll do, but she's not going to be nice about anything that she doesn't approve of."

"We'll have to wait and see." He nodded as if he knew that was what he was going to say. "You can live here, the two of you. The bed isn't too old, but it works better than a floor. Also, as you said, it has a kitchen that you can use. When you decide to move in, I'll spot you some money for food so that you can cook at home."

He started crying again. The man was so emotional sometimes that his heart hurt for him. As they were closing up the place, he handed him the key when Allen said he was going to stay there tonight so he'd be ready for work in the morning. He told him about the job that he had for his wife, too, if she wanted to work.

"I'll tell her. I don't know what she'll do, but I'm going to tell her what a good man you are to work for." Melbourne thanked him, and they went their separate ways. He had a feeling that it was going to be just Allen living in the back portion of the house while Belinda fussed about having to live in an abandoned house without heat or any place to cook. Not that he thought that she would be cooking all that much.

~*~

Allen was excited to have a good roof over his head. He was also happy that he'd be able to have a place to cook a meal when it was time for supper. Now all he had to do was talk to Belinda and see how she was going to react. He didn't look for it to go well.

She was napping when he got back to their place. Since they didn't have anything but the clothing on their backs, they could just go to the house and move in. Allen was going to get him some much-needed shirts when he got paid on Friday. There were other things that he could use, but he wasn't sure what his check was going to be. He'd not had one in more years than he could count.

Deciding to just tell her what was going on and not beating around the bush about it, he watched her face when he told her where their new place was going to be. He didn't know if they'd be paying rent for the rooms, but he decided to ask Melbourne first thing in the morning.

"What do you mean, it's just a couple of rooms with a bed. You expect me to sleep on someone else's mattress?" He told her that anything was better than sleeping on the cold floor. "I don't know. Just a couple of rooms? How are we supposed to live in that small of a place? I don't want to be crowded around."

"You shared a room with fifty other women in prison. I'd think you'd like just having a couple of rooms to yourself for a change. And it has a kitchen in it that we can save money by cooking our meals instead of going out all the time."

"I'm not going to be cooking anything, Allen. It's too much work to get finished then to clean up. No, we'll eat out all the time because we don't want to have a mess when we have to live in such small accommodations." He didn't mention cooking again, and she seemed to be all right with that. "Where is this place? And what do we have to do for rent money? You've not even told me what you'll be doing when we live there."

"I'll be doing the same thing that I'm doing now. There's no change in my job. I'll have to ask Melbourne what the rent will be, but he's a fair man and I'm sure it won't be much." He looked around the room that they'd been sharing. "It's close to downtown, so we can walk wherever we want to go. The library is just a block away, and the store is just another couple of blocks down the street. We will have neighbors, too, that we can make friends with."

"You've already told him that we'd take it, I assume." He asked her why they'd give up something that they could live in over being in an abandoned home. "I'll have to see it before I decide to move in. And if it's not up to my standards, what will he give us to go someplace else?"

"There isn't anyplace else to go. I asked him about the place and he said we could stay there. And I'm going to even if you decide that you don't want to." She asked him what he'd said. "You heard me. I'm sick of living here and sleeping on the floor. I'm going to go to the place tonight and sleep there. I think it will be nicer than staying here and sleeping on the floor, don't you?"

"I'll have to see it. But if it's too small or dirty, he'll have to get us something better. I'm not taking something that's going to need a lot of work to make it livable." He asked her if she wanted to go now. "Now? Why are you in such a hurry? There isn't any reason for us to go tonight. I'm betting either the rent is going to be too high or the place is going to be infested with some kind of bugs. I won't have it, Allen. We might as well stay here if he's going to be unreasonable. Just tell him we want something bigger than just a couple of rooms. That'll be all right with me."

"I'm going back over there tonight so I can have a warm shower in the morning and sleep in a good bed." She told him he was not. "I am. You just want to complain about everything. Remember what our parole officer said, we needed to establish ourselves in a residence, or we'll be put in the halfway house somewhere else. I like being here, where I have a job and get to see my daughters once in a while."

"What are they going to think when we invite them over and don't have enough room to turn around in? I'm sure that will make them want to not help us." He told her that he didn't want his daughters to bail them out. "Why not? They're the reason that we were in prison in the first place. The least they can do is take care of us."

"You mean like we did them? I think we'll be lucky if they want anything to do with us after the way we treated them." She said that they'd paid for their crime. "Only if it isn't something that we do again will they have anything to do with us. I'm sure of it."

"You've been talking to them, haven't you?" He admitted that he'd had lunch with them today. "Lunch again? How dare you? And how dare they want to have lunch with you and not me?"

"I didn't set it up. Melbourne did when he bought me lunch; he invited them over to have lunch with us, too. It was a very tense meeting. And Justine is so afraid that I'm going to hurt her again, she could barely eat her lunch. I promised them that I'd never hurt them again." She asked him why he'd do that. "Because I don't want to hurt them either one again. They're good women with a job and education, too. I enjoyed just learning about them and what they'd been up to. Did you know that Sammy went to college and got a business management degree? And Justine works from home doing stuffing mail envelopes for companies. We should be proud of them for what they accomplished."

"You bastard." He didn't understand where that had come from and stepped back when she looked as if she was going to hit him. "First, you tell them that you're not going to be hurting them anymore to make me the bad guy. What if that's the only way we can get anything out of them? Did you ever think of that? Then secondly, you want to shame us by living in a too small building on someone else's mattress while they're no doubt living the high life. Did you even bother to demand money from them, did you?"

"Why would I ask them for money when I have a job on my own? Also, there is one for you, too, if you want to take it." Belinda said that there was no way she was going to take a job out of pity. "There's something wrong with you. I'll ask you this again: we have to have a place to live before we see our parole officer again, or they'll take us out of here. That's including a job each. What are you going to do if you don't have a job and he makes you go to a halfway house? Because I have a job and I like it. I'm not going to do anything that I'm not supposed to do to keep seeing my daughters."

"Well, laud dee da for you." He asked her what that was supposed to mean. "It means that if I have to go to a halfway house, then so will you. You're my husband, and I demand that you get money from our kids so that we don't have to work anymore. You must look like a fool walking up and down the street marking things on a map. I won't do anything. I'm not working either. If you're so cozy up with our daughters—not just yours but ours—then you get money from them before I have to beat you too."

"They're not going to help you at all if you don't behave around them." She said that she would make them pay for sending her to prison. "Then I wish you luck with your life, Belinda. I'm going to go live in that place because it's better than living here with no roof over our head and no running hot water."

He turned to leave and felt her move rather than see her. When she shoved him down the stairs, he was headed down to go away. His last thought was that he was going to die, and he'd never gotten his daughters to trust him. Christ, he didn't want to die.

Chapter 6

Sammy liked this house, but she was bored looking at houses that were bigger than she could afford. When she'd offered half of the amount they'd be paying for the house, Melbourne had said he had it covered, but she insisted. Now she was regretting not just letting him pay for the whole thing. And they'd have to start from scratch, too, in order to move into a house rather than the condos that both of them had.

"It has six bedrooms, not including the master suite, and five full baths as well as three half baths." That was a great deal of house, she thought to herself, but the relator continued. "There is a family room as well as a living room that is set up for large families. The pool out back is nice too and has been used until recently." Melbourne asked her what she thought.

"It's very large." He said that he had a big family. "They're not living with us, are they? I mean, they have their own homes, correct?"

He laughed. "Yes, they do. I just meant that when they come over, we won't have to crowd up in one room where we can watch sports on television. I never asked, but do you like fall sports?" She told him that she loved football. "Good, so do I. We usually meet at my parents' home and watch it there, but I think I'd like to have them over here sometimes to watch and pig out on snack food. Do you like to cook?"

"I've never been one to cook, no. But I can if pressed. I usually get my meals from the restaurant, so I don't have to mess with it." Instead of being mad like she thought he would, he told her she was brilliant at working around that way. He would, too, if he owned a place that served food like they did there. "Does anything bother you? I said I don't cook, and you took that as it was all right. I mentioned that I don't like to keep house, and you said it would be all right because we'd have staff. Do you ever get upset?"

"Not since I met you, I don't. I don't see the reason for getting all tied up in bunches just because you'd rather not cook. There are more important things than getting pissed off because you don't like to dust. I don't either. For either one. I can cook too when I have to, but I work full time and so do you, so there isn't any way that we're going to have time for cooking us a meal at the end of a busy work day." She blurted out that she didn't have enough money for a house that big. He pulled her aside and into a dark bedroom. "As much as I'd like to kiss you right now, I have to make something clear to you. I have more than enough money for us to have whatever we want and have enough left over to give every man, woman, and child in town a million dollars. I don't know if I mentioned this, but I've been around for a very long time and have been able to save billions of dollars since I was old enough to get out of the house. And the thing about dragon tears is true. I have, in addition to money, a great many gems that I've saved over the years, too. I want you to be happy. That's my sole purpose in life: to make you happier every day that we're alive. And that's going to be for a good long time, too. Understand?"

She nodded. "I'm still worried that you'll find someone else better than me to hang on your arm." He laughed and told her that he'd have to be a dead man if he were to find someone better than she was. "You're serious, aren't you? You actually believe that we're going to be together for the rest of our lives."

"The rest of our lives and beyond, love. And in all those days, I'm going to do my damndest to make you happier every day that we're together. Also, to tell you how much more I love you today than I did yesterday, and will love you more on the morrow. And if you want to have children with me, they'll be just as happy as you because I will make sure they are. They'll also know that they're loved, too." She told him not to spoil the children. "Never that. We'll raise them to know value. Of work and of money. I swear that I'll only spoil them a little when they come along and that will be enough."

The rest of the tour of the house they were in went much better. But they didn't put an offer in on this home. It was too small in the yard. He wanted a large yard so that he could shift and lay about in the grass. She couldn't wait to see his dragon. It didn't matter to her how big he was; she was going to enjoy seeing her first dragon of her life.

The next house, they both liked, but held off on making an offer. It was all right with its six bedrooms again, but it was the yard again that kept them from buying the home. The realtor said that they should buy some land and have a house built on it. They might consider that if nothing else was coming to them.

The last house they looked at was the winner all the way around. It had seven bedrooms in it and six full baths. They were talking about putting a half bath down the hall from the kitchen, but they were just looking for now. The yard was tremendous, and it had a high-fenced backyard with a pool and plenty of room for him to shift if he wanted. He loved that most of all. Sammy liked that there were two offices on the main floor, and they didn't have to share one. She didn't have an office in her condo and wished she had. Even the kitchen had been updated recently, and they both appreciated that as well.

Just as they were going over the specs of the

house with Ms. James, the relator, his cell phone rang. He was surprised to be hearing from Allen because he thought he'd be in the house by now. Instead, there had been an accident.

"She pushed me down the stairs." He asked him if he was all right. "I don't know. I hit my head hard on the stairs. I don't know where Belinda is, but I've called an ambulance. She pushed me down the stairs, Melbourne. Why would she do that?"

"I'm on my way to see you now. Actually, we'll meet you at the hospital. You just hang in there." He told Sammy what was going on, and she was ready to leave right then. "I just have to take care of one thing, and we'll meet you in the emergency room. I'll pick up Justine on the way."

"Thank you. I don't know what was in her head." He said that they'd take care of it. "All right. Just tell the girls that I'm all right. I have a lot of blood on me from the head wound, but I think I'm going to be all right." The ambulance arrived just as he was telling him that they'd be careful.

They put an offer in on the house because they didn't want to lose it. After signing the papers, Sammy called her sister to be picked up, and they made their way to her house. She lived in the condo units where Sammy did, but Justine didn't know that she owned the area. When she got into the car, she looked like she'd been crying, and Melbourne decided to just drive and let them talk between themselves. He had a lot on his mind anyway, with Belinda shoving Allen down the stairs. What was wrong with her head in doing something like that, he wondered too.

The ambulance was just pulling in when they arrived. They had his leg in a splint because they'd told him that they thought it might be broken. As he was rushed off to have tests done on his head and leg, the three of them waited in his room. It was going to be a long night, he thought, and asked Sammy what she wanted to do about their mother pushing their father down the stairs.

"We'll wait and see what he wants to do. They might have been having a fight, and that's what happened, or he could have tripped thinking that Mom pushed him. There are just too many things that could be wrong about this. Don't you think?" He agreed with Sammy, and Justine said it was something that their mother did when she was upset. Just shove someone down; it didn't matter if it was stairs or not, she'd just push a person down to prove her point. Whatever that was.

His leg was indeed broken, and it was starting to pain him quite a bit when he got back from X-ray. As they were giving him something for pain, he started telling them what they'd been talking about when she got mad. Melbourne said that he was afraid something like this would happen; he was just glad that he'd given him a cell phone so that he could call 911. Otherwise, there would have been no way to know how much longer he would have been lying there bleeding and in pain.

"I don't know where she was when I left the place. I was unconscious for some time, I think." Sammy asked her dad if he thought that she pushed him or had she just fallen into him when he was near the stairs. "No, she pushed me. I remember hearing her laughing and saying that would teach me to disagree with her. I'd forgotten about that part of her. She didn't like to be told no either."

"It'll be fine. We'll take care of everything." Justine startled her by saying that to their dad, and she wondered if her feelings had changed. "You just concentrate on getting better, and we'll make sure that you're safe."

"Thank you both so much for coming in tonight." He cried himself to sleep; the drugs were finally making his pain a lot more bearable. As he laid there on the gurney, Sammy wondered where her mother was. Not that she cared if she was all right, but just so she'd not hurt her dad anymore. Things about her mom were coming out that she didn't think she cared about right now.

Sammy told her sister about the house that she was buying with Melbourne. Justine seemed to be excited about it, but she did worry that they'd not known one another very long, and she wondered if this was the right thing to do. After assuring her that she thought she would fall in love with Melbourne soon, Justine just nodded. She didn't need her to be negative right now, and it was getting on her nerves.

"If you're moving out of your condo, do you think that they'd care if I moved into yours? You have those lovely front windows that I love, as well as that small room off from the bedroom. It would be the perfect size for me to do my work in. Not big enough for a full office, but enough for what I need it for." She said they could ask, knowing that it would be a done deal if that was what she really wanted. "I could sell my condo, then give you the money for yours if that's all right. I really love those front windows that you have that look out over the front lawn."

"It's doubtful that anyone would care so long as we didn't." She said that would be great, and Sammy wondered if it was time for her to tell her sister that she owned the entire place. After she did, her sister stared at her. "I've owned it for a good long time. Even before you moved in, so if it would help you, I've enough money now that you could live in either place for free from now on."

"That's a lot of money that I'd not be paying for a condo. Can you really afford that?" She said that since she was buying a house with Melbourne, she had extra cash as he was wealthy enough to afford to pay cash for the house they were buying. "I heard that they all have money and wondered what would happen when you moved out. I guess you hit the jackpot."

"I did in that he says that he's falling in love with me." Justine just sat there, not saying anything else, and Sammy let her. If she was mad, she was all right with that, too. It had been a big secret to keep from her, and she might well have been mad too if the roles were reversed. When Dad woke up, he told them the same story about how Mom had pushed him down the stairs and how he'd hit his head pretty hard. "You should call the police."

"Oh, I don't know. Won't that make her madder? I don't need her to be pissy with me right now while I'm healing." Sammy said that it was better than him being dead at the bottom of the stairs. "I actually thought of that when I was going down. How I didn't want to die while falling down when I'd just gotten myself a place to stay and my daughters were talking to me."

"I think you should think about it, Allen. If she thinks she can get by with it this time, there is no telling what she'll do in the future. Besides that, she left you on the stairs to die, and that's not a good thing." Dad said he'd think about it when he wasn't in so much pain. "They said you can have more before they put you in a cast. I'll even go out and tell them that you're ready for some more pain medication."

Dad fell asleep again after the meds were given to him. The nurse said it was a good thing that it was knocking him out so that he'd be rested when he went home in a couple of days. His leg was broken in two places, the doctor had said, and that he wasn't going to be able to be alone until he could get around better. Melbourne said he'd take care that he had care someplace that he'd like.

Sammy couldn't believe how much Melbourne was doing for her dad. He'd given him a job and found him a place to live. When Dad had asked about the hospital stay, he'd also told him that it would be taken care of, too, as he worked for him. Dad couldn't have been working for him that long, yet Melbourne said that he had insurance as well as paid time off. She was really beginning to like her new mate if he was this nice to near strangers.

~*~

It didn't take long for them to have things just the way he needed them to be. Melbourne had put Allen in his condo and had hired a staff to take care of him. Even though the thought of being homeless himself, Melbourne thought that this was the best solution that they could all live with. He was taken care of, and no one was out of their own lives, making sure that Allen was all right.

The offer on the house was approved, and they now owned a home. All they had to do now was outfit it into a house with furniture, then they'd be set. He had made arrangements to take Sammy on a shopping spree on Tuesday, which was in two more days. It was the only day that she could get off from the restaurant, and they were going to spend the entire day getting what they needed to be able to move into the house right away. It was empty but for the furniture that had been used to set up the house so that it didn't look empty, and that should only take them a day or two to get out.

"I've made a list of things that we have to have to move in. Most of it's stuff for the bedrooms and the living room. I know we don't need the living room right away, but to be honest with you, I'd like a place I can go to after work and just chill. My living room was a makeshift office for when I worked from home on Mondays and Thursdays." Sammy looked up at him. "How did I get so lucky in finding you when I didn't know that I needed you?"

"We were both just lucky, I guess." He kissed her on the nose, and she smiled at him. "I could live off your smiles at me for a long time. You're very beautiful when you look at me like that."

"I have a queen-sized bed at my condo that's not getting much use right now." He told her he was sorry for keeping her up so late talking. "I meant that we could go there and have some sex later if you want. I'm sick of waiting around for the right moment to have sex with you. If you're willing, that is."

"Willing? I'd say I've been willing since I met you." She laughed, and he told her that he was serious. "I've fallen in love with you since the day I met you. And each day that I'm with you means that I've fallen in love with you more."

"I love you too. I didn't think it was possible, but I woke up this morning and thought of all the things you've done for me in keeping me safe and that of my family. It's more to it than that, but I wanted you to know that I've never been so happy as I am right now." He kissed her again, deepening the kiss so that she could tell how much he loved her. Pulling her into his arms, he pulled her body flush to his and let her know his body when she was near him. Lifting his head, he decided that he was going to make love to her all night if he could. She was his everything.

It took them for what seemed forever to get back to her condo. They would stop every few steps and kiss or hold one another. It was the most romantic walk he'd ever taken with someone. Especially not his brothers, he thought with a laugh. Holding her hand as he drove, he hated to let it go when he had to shift gears. There was just so much warmth in her body that he found that he didn't want to let her go, even for a second.

Her condo was bigger than his in that the living room was attached to a dining area. He had an eat-in kitchen that he didn't use all that much, but it was there when he needed to clean up after a meal that he had brought home from work. He was glad that he had a service come in once a week to clean up after him, or it might well have not worked out with Allen living there. So far, it was going well for the older man.

Once they were at the condo, however, they both kind of went their separate ways, in that they seemed embarrassed about being there just to have sex. He asked her about her place, and she told him that it was a done deal that her sister was going to take her place over her own.

"She loves the windows." He said that he could enjoy them too, but they let in a lot of sunlight. "That's the problem I had with them. They made a glare on the television when I would try to watch it. Finally, I just took the thing to my bedroom and watched what I wanted in there. Which, as you can well imagine, wasn't all that often."

"Yes, I understand. I rarely watch television at

my place for about the same reasons. Not the glare, but the lack of room on the walls for it to hang. I got sick of it being on my coffee table all the time, so I just stopped watching it. I usually end up at one of my brother's homes when I want to watch something like a game. They usually have a lot of food too when they're having me over." She asked him if that was why he was excited to have them over to their home. "It is. So that I can return the favor of watching television with them. And of course, have a nice spread of food."

"You guys do eat a lot. I've noticed that you usually have a couple of meals each when you go out. That's a lot of food." He said that they were a lot of dragon. "I'd like to see him someday. Speaking of which, I've a dragon like you told me that I would. He's on my back most of the time. I'm glad you told me about him. I might well have freaked out worse than I did when I felt him moving on my body."

"He's there to protect you from harm. Once we have sex and bond, then he'll be bigger and be able to lift you out of situations where you might well be harmed." She said that she was glad for that. "I am as well. Even though you're immortal, you can still be hurt, and that wouldn't be good to have to live with whatever happened if you were to be hurt badly."

"I find myself to be more aware of my surroundings. Like I'm always on the lookout for something that could harm me. Especially with my mom out there doing whatever she's been doing. I can't believe that she pushed my dad down the stairs. Though now that I say that out loud, I don't know why I expected anything less from her." He told her that she was at the building again now, and he had a faerie on her at all times. "Good. Having a heads up would be nice if she was planning on coming around to hurt one of us. I have a feeling that she's going to search Justine and me out for something that we're not willing to give her. Money mostly, and a place to live. I have no desire to help her out at all."

"Pancake is watching over her, and he said that she talks to herself a great deal. Was that something she did before?" Sammy told him that was how they figured out what she had planned for them when she would do that. "I thought as much. She's very comfortable with it. Like she's making sure that she's right all the time—or justified in what she's doing to get herself what she wants."

"That sounds like her." Sammy went into the kitchen area and turned to look at him while she stood at the counter. "I thought that I wanted to have sex with you. I'm now thinking that I just need a place to be warmed by you. Don't be mad at me. I didn't mean to lead you on. But with all this talk about my parents, all I can think about is how they treated us as children, and Mom is doing the same thing again."

"She'll not harm you, Sammy. Not so long as I have my dragon." She nodded, but he could tell that she wasn't convinced. He didn't blame her; there was no way to just forget about that many years of abuse and come out all right. "And I'm not mad at all. Whatever you need, I'm here for you. And if all you want is to cuddle all night, I'm here for you, too."

He watched as she seemed to be crying. Moving toward her, he pulled her into his arms and held her to him. There was no way that he was going to be able to stand for her to hurt like this and not hold her to him. As she turned in his arms and held onto him, the tears came then. The great sobs that he thought she'd been holding in for so long were coming out. He loved this woman and felt the bitterness that he felt for her parents; both of them came through in that moment.

"My dad is trying so hard, isn't he?" He said that he seemed to want this to work out. "He does, and Mom pushed him down the stairs. I have no doubt that she did that either. She pushed me down the stairs quite often when I was a child. Justine too. She's mean and cruel, and while I know she's my mom, I can't stand to be around her anymore. I hate her."

He held onto her until he picked her up and made his way to her bedroom. Lying her down while she still cried, his heart hurt for her, and he pulled off his shirt and pants. He was trying to think of something to say to her that he'd not said a hundred times before about her mom, but he couldn't think of anything. Instead, he got in bed with her and was glad that she curled around him, holding him as tightly as he held her.

He woke sometime in the middle of the night, and with the darkened room, he didn't know where he was. Instead of getting up when he figured it out, he noticed that her side of the bed, while warm, was empty. She was just getting back in the bed when he decided to go and find her.

"I hate how cold this room is. And I've turned off the air conditioner." She snuggled up to him, and he held onto her shaking body. "I love you, Melbourne. Thanks for staying with me."

"I love you." He laughed when she elbowed him twice before settling down. "This might be a big enough bed for one person, but certainly not for the two of us. You get comfy, and I'll get that way around you."

He noticed that she'd put on something other than the jeans and sweatshirt she'd had on. The flannel pajamas were super soft and smelled like her. Melbourne held her tightly until she was out again, and he laid there thinking about the day that he was going to have tomorrow. He was going to convince

Allen to press charges against his wife.

If the girls thought it was a good idea. He nearly forgot that he had to take their feelings into consideration. He would have done it himself but for the fact that they all seemed to be giving her a second chance. Melbourne wasn't into second chances with people who nearly killed someone by pushing them down the stairs. He wanted justice, and he wanted it now.

The sun was nearly up when he woke. The room was dusted in a nice mauve color that he thought suited the room nicely. He could see the furniture now and wasn't surprised that everything on the dresser was neat as a pen, and the closet door was open, too, where the same neatness was. He liked his things neat, too, and thought that they'd get along nicely when it came to sharing a room. He looked down at her when she snored softly.

Melbourne couldn't believe that the beauty in his arms was his. He'd thought of finding a mate nearly all his adult life and wondered who she would be. There were times, too, that he feared never having someone to love; it had been years and years since he'd become an adult. But with Sammy here and now, all he could think about was the years that they'd have together, making memories together, and perhaps having children too to make even more memories with.

When she finally woke up, he smiled at her. Her bright smile made his heart beat a little faster for the closeness of the two of them. As soon as she kissed him on the chin, he kissed her back, deepening the kiss just enough that she knew that he loved her.

"I have so much to do today. I have to order for the restaurant. Do payroll for the employees. Then I have to see about getting out of here so that my sister can move in." Her whispered comment had him grinning bigger. "If we didn't get up, do you think anyone would care?"

"I wouldn't care a bit if we were to lie here all day and never venture out." She giggled, and he laughed with her. "Of course, the restaurant wouldn't have any food next week, and people might not get paid. I can see your sister trying to find you if she backs up with a moving truck and you're still in bed."

"Yeah, I guess we should get up." But she didn't move, and he was all right with that. "We really should get up before I fall asleep again. I think that was the first night I've slept so well in a long time. At least since my parents got out of prison. I'm also going to see him today to tell him to press charges against Mom." He said that he'd been thinking the same thing. "Can you do that for me? Help him get her into jail before she hurts anyone else?"

"It'll be my pleasure. I have some things to do

myself. Not as much as you do, but I do have some contracts to go over and furniture to purchase." She said she'd forgotten about that. "We'll get to it, no worries. If anything, we can find us a nice house to rent until the house is ready. All right?"

They both got up then but played around in the bedroom until they both had a shower. He pulled on his clothing and decided that he needed to go to his own place to pack up, too. There was a lot going on, and he found that he was all right with it. He had a mate and everything was making him happy nowadays.

Chapter 7

Everyone had clocked in correctly and had actually clocked out the same way. Payroll only took her about half the time because she didn't have to chase people down and ask them what they worked on certain days. Since she'd already finished up the order for next week, she gave herself a little treat by leaving her office with her desk covered in paperwork. She went to find Donald, her cook and friend.

"You look like you're happy." She told him about payroll and how she'd gotten the order finished up as well. "Good for you. I bet you even remembered that we'll be closed on Monday of next week because I'll be out of state."

"I did remember that. And I've put the day of vacation on this check for you so that you'd have extra money, like you asked for when you got to your sister's. See? I do pay attention." They both laughed, and he asked her if she'd gotten laid last night. "No, not that it's any of your business, but I might soon. We're just without a house right now, and it's making things difficult. Justine is going to take my condo and sell hers, so I'm having my place packed up right now."

"You told me that." She nodded and asked if he had anything that she could munch on. He handed her a plate of carrots and celery that he was chopping up, and she sat down on the chair next to the stove where he was working. "I've been thinking about you and your parents. What are you going to do if they come in here and start making an issue? If they're following you around, it wouldn't take anything for them to follow you here."

"It's just my mom I'm worried about." She told him about how she had pushed her dad down the stairs when he didn't do something that she wanted. "Melbourne is going to see my dad today and convince him that he needs to press charges. There is no telling how long he would have laid there if he'd not had a phone to call for help. And in order for her to have left the building that they're staying in, she would have had to have stepped right over him to get out."

"That's cold." She agreed as he put cauliflower on her plate along with some strips of pepper that he was cutting up for dinner tonight. "What does your mate think about—I've been meaning to ask you about him for the last week. Do we know him?"

"You might have heard of him at the very least. He's with the Walsh family. His name is Melbourne. You remember me talking about Alex and Storm Walsh before? They're the richest people in the country,

I've heard." He whistled and she nodded at him. "Melbourne and I bought a house the other day, and he debated on paying cash for it. That's more money than I've got right now." It wasn't, but Donald didn't have to know that right now.

After finishing her snack, she was ready to get back to work. Going back to her office, she pulled her phone to her and called Melbourne. She could do the mind thingy, but she wanted to talk to him like this. In person would have been better, but she was happy that they could talk on the phone.

"I just left your dad. He's going to be pressing charges. There will be a warrant out for her arrest, and she'll be picked up soon. If nothing else, they can find her at the building where she has been staying." She asked him how her dad felt about that. "He told me as soon as I was in his room that he'd been thinking about doing just that. He also said that he's afraid of her and doesn't want to have to look over his shoulder all the time while laid up the way that he is."

"You've been busy. So have I." She told him what she'd been able to accomplish, and he told her that he was proud of her. "Also, I called in a mover and am having my place emptied and things put into storage until I can get it into the house. Are we still on for tomorrow? I'm excited to go shopping with you."

"Yes, if something comes up, I've got my

brothers covering for me. I don't foresee anything coming up, but you never know. They know how it is to move into a house with nothing more than the shirt on your back." She told him that she still had the list of things that they needed. "Mom said that you should think about each room and go over using it. Then you can decide if you've gotten everything or not."

"I've even gone over some of the things that I had in my condo to know what to get. The one thing that I remembered to write down was towels. We're going to need a lot of towels with us both working." He said that his mom was interviewing lots of people who could work for them, and she had a list of people that they could interview. "I guess you're right in us having staff. I've never had any before, so you'll have to help me out with that."

"It's nothing to it. You just hire someone who is in charge of what they need to be doing, and it gets done." She said that made sense. "Mom said to make sure we hire as many pack that is around to help us out. They could use the income, and the entire pack could use the work as they're a smallish pack."

"I have some of the pack working for me now. Or I guess us. I'm going to have to put that on my list of things to do, which is to get you on the paperwork of the things that I own." He said that he had her an appointment with the bank first thing in the morning.

"Good. I don't know what it'll take for you to get onto mine, but I don't own that much. I would imagine that you have a lot of things that you own."

"We do." They talked about what they were going to be doing for the rest of the day, and she told him that she needed to get to it. Just as she was going up front to open for the day, three cruisers pulled up in front of the building across the street from her and went into it. She paused in opening the front door. The police were going to be in for a big surprise if they thought that she was going to come in easily.

They were in there for a lot longer than she thought they should have been, but when they came out, they were taking her mom to one of the cruisers that had been there. She had her hands behind her, so she could only assume that she had been handcuffed, and Sammy actually felt some of her anxiety roll off her shoulders. It was nice to know that she was in jail or soon would be.

For the rest of the day and into the evening, she ran errands and made a deposit to the bank when the lunch rush was over. As she was putting the things away on her desk, she added several more things to her list of things to get tomorrow and was glad that she had thought of them. It wouldn't do them a lick of good to have a house without having the locks changed and extra keys made for it. She was just getting ready to leave for the night when Donald reminded her again that she had to give him the menu for tomorrow's special.

"You do it. I know you know me well enough that I'm not going to have a problem with whatever you make. Just check with me on the price, and we'll be fine." He told her that he was thinking of using the extra salmon and making salmon patties for lunch with hollandaise sauce, then for supper, they'd have beef tips. He gave her a price on both items. "Sounds good. Especially the hollandaise sauce on the patties. That's one of my favorites that you make."

"I know that." She told him to call her when they closed, and she'd come in and do the paperwork. "I'll do that. You need to hire an assistant to help you out when you want a day off. You're working too hard as it is. Just hire someone already."

"I keep thinking that I need to, but the thought of having to train someone on what I do every day is too daunting. Some days, when I come in here, it's overwhelming, the crap that I have to do to keep this place running." He asked her if she was thinking of quitting the restaurant altogether. "No. Not that. I might hire someone, as you said, but I won't quit. This is my baby, and I love her too much to just hand her over to someone else who might run her into the ground. No, I'm not quitting."

After leaving for the day, she got a text message from Melbourne to meet her at the bed and breakfast. They had things to go over. All for getting things out of the way for tomorrow, she made her way there just after she made it to the bank to sign papers. As she was driving over, she had one thought in her head. Getting the house ready for them to be able to live in. However, as soon as she opened the door to the room she was to go to, she thought of being made love to tonight. The room was magnificent.

There were flower petals on the floor up to the bed, which was filled with different colored roses all over the pillows and blankets. There were two fluted glasses with a bottle in an icy bucket that she thought was champagne on one of the bedside tables. She could see a basket of fruit that held apples and grapes, a charcuterie with meats and cheeses on it, and a small basket full of crackers. Stepping into the room, she could see other things around that reminded her of romance and sex.

The drapes were closed, and the room smelled of fresh roses. There was a television on, but instead of something on it like a show, it was a roaring fireplace with the sounds of crackling wood burning. Moving deeper into the room, looking for Melbourne, she found him coming out of the bathroom dressed in a robe of dark blood red velvet, if she wasn't mistaken.

And he looked as handsome as ever, she thought.

"I thought that we'd have a good time tonight." She couldn't help it, she burst out laughing. "I've gone to a lot of trouble. Please tell me what you find so funny."

"This is all so romantic, and you come out with a line about having a good time. Like we're going to be swinging from the ceiling fan or something." She looked up at the fan and decided that it was just too small for anything like that. "You did go to a lot of trouble, and I love it. You're very romantic, aren't you?"

"My dad is too. And over the years, I've been watching him. He would buy flowers for Mom when there was no reason other than that he loved her. Sometimes, once a week or so, they go out on a date night. Even when we were children." He took two steps toward her. "I've come to realize that for this moment in time, I couldn't love you any more than I do right now. And in a few minutes, I'll love you even more."

"You had me at the flowers on the floor." She moved toward him and smiled. "I love you, Melbourne. So very much. You're like the sun shining on my face on a beautiful day. Like the breath in my body when I think I have no other reason to breathe. You're my everything in this world forever and a day."

"I love you so much, Sammy. And like you, I know that I'm going to love you for all reasons from now until eternity. Now they were within touching distance of each other, and she reached out her fingers and ran them down the opening of his robe. "I thought about this moment forever, it seems. Getting to make love to my one and only heart."

When they kissed, it was like everything in her body opened up for him. Her heart beat a bit faster, and her breath caught. When he opened the buttons on her blouse, she watched his face as he pulled her blouse off and dropped it to the floor.

"Are you naked beneath that robe?" He grinned and told her that he was. That he'd not wanted to waste time in undressing when she got here. "I like the way you think, my dear heart. Let me see what you have beneath that wonderful piece of clothing."

Instead of allowing her to disrobe him, he pulled her pants off to her hips. When he got down on his knees in front of her, removing her pants as he went, Sammy had several tiny climaxes when he kissed his way from her knee to her hip. Then it was onto her navel, where he made love to it with his mouth and tongue.

~*~

Sitting back on his knees, he looked up at the goddess before him. She was perfect. To him, there wasn't a flaw on her. As he took in her scent, the sweet nectar of her pussy, he inhaled deeply before leaning forward and kissing her just below her navel and above her pussy. She shuddered out a hard climax as he took again in her scent as she filled his nostrils.

For as much as he wanted to taste her, he wanted to make love to her more. She was his everything, and he wanted to lay claim to her now. As she stood before him, he walked her backwards toward the bed, and when she bumped into it, she sat down. Standing up was one of the hardest things he'd ever done when all he wanted to do was spread her out and taste every morsel of her.

Standing up, he towered over her. Kissing her from that height gave him all kinds of views of her body, and he crawled into bed with her. She was beneath him when he wrapped his arms around her and took her hands to the top of the bed. There, he held them so that he could explore without her distracting him. Christ, she was so beautiful.

When he brought his hands down to her hips, she rolled over on top of him until he was on his back. With her over him, she straddled both his legs and leaned down to kiss the skin that had been exposed by his robe opening. When she got to his navel, she did the same thing he'd done and made love to it as he'd done to hers. It was by and far the most erotic thing that he'd had done to himself in forever.

After exposing his cock, she asked him to remove her panties. The only way that he could think to do that was to rip them off her. Putting his hands on either side of them, he yanked them apart with some of the strength of his dragon. Her climax nearly did him in.

It was a screaming climax that had her laying her head on his abdomen, where her breath blew across his cock. It was hot and moist, blowing across him; he nearly whimpered, causing him to close his eyes and hope that he could hang onto his sanity, at the very least, his manhood.

When she sat up, her body limp looking, and weak, he helped her to sit on his cock and ride him. There were no words that he could think of to describe the sensations that went from the bottom of his feet to the top of his head. Nothing could have prepared him for the tightness of her sheath nor the smooth drive into her. As he laid there panting, his breath coming out in short, hard punches to his system, he thought of anything but where he was and what he was doing. In bed with the love of his life while making love to her.

She rode him in long, smooth movements. Each time her hips pressed down onto him, he surged upwards to get deeper inside of her. With each stroke of his cock inside of her, he had to hold onto her hips or he was going to shatter.

Sitting up, he removed her bra, one of the tiniest things he'd ever seen, so that he could have access to her wonderful breasts. Her nipples were small but hard and long. He sampled them both, one at a time, while she fucked him like she was. Pulling her closer to him, he was ready to come, to fill her with his seed, when he was rolled over again and onto his back. With her beneath him, he fucked her harder as he held her tighter to his body. He touched parts of her, her breast, hips, and ass, that he'd never gotten to touch before today. Christ, he thought, when he came, he was going to be lucky if he didn't die; his body was so stiff and hard, ready to come when she did.

With her legs wrapped around his hips, he knew she was getting the most out of their fucking. Licking a path from her throat to her ear, he tasted more of her skin until he could find her with only a small breath from her. Licking along the pounding pulse, he felt her shudder just a little, and when he bit down on her throat, he was rewarded with not just her coppery-tasting blood but the very essence of her. Then she stiffened beneath him.

"Come." She screamed out his name. Screaming over and over until he knew she was going to be hoarse from it. Watching her face, her beautiful face, while she came was all he could do while she came four, five, six times as he held her to him. Then suddenly his own body came, and he couldn't have described it any better than his entire body came with her, just as they were supposed to do as a mated couple.

Melbourne came twice more as he laid atop of her. His body was spent, but seemed to know there was just enough of him left to come a few more times before he was finished. Rolling to his side, leaving Sammy where she lay, he couldn't have stopped the tremors from wracking his body if he had tried. It was all he could do not to break his teeth as he shuddered from the impact that his releases had on him. It was the most powerful climax that he'd ever had in all his life, and he was humbled that one small human mate had done him in.

At some point, he woke up and had to use the bathroom. He was turned around in the room and didn't know where his bathroom was for a moment until he got his bearings. Once he was finished and had washed his hands, he limped back to the bed after stubbing his toe on the side of the door jam coming out. Sammy was right where he had left her and climbed into bed without disturbing her much.

The second time he woke, the room was flooded with bright sunshine. He'd closed the drapes, but it must have been later than he'd thought. Sammy was still sleeping, for which he was happy, and he made his way to the bathroom for a second time. This time, he managed not to hurt himself but made it back to bed in time for his alarm to go off. He'd forgotten to turn it off when he didn't have to work. Sammy rolled to her side and looked at him.

"Don't touch me." He let go of a burst of laughter that had him smiling when asking her what had happened. "I feel like my fingers have found an electrical outlet here under the covers, and I'm buzzing. It could be the most incredible sex anyone has ever had before, but whatever it is, I'm too hyped up to have you touching me."

"All right. I won't touch you. But I will admit this only to you. I feel like I've been shocked with paddles as well. Just like my entire body had been subject to some kind of wonderful abuse, and it doesn't know how to react to it." Sammy nodded. "All I want to do is go back to sleep so that my body can calm down enough where I won't embarrass myself when I have to go out into the real world."

"How many days are we staying here?" He told her for the next week. "If we have sex like we just did again, I'm going to be pushing up daisies, I kid you not. I'm pretty sure that I used muscles that I've never used before during that, and I have to admit that I ache a little from it. I'm not saying it was bad, not at all, but I'm going to be sore when I get up and I have to really pee."

"I'm sorry." But his laughter at her had her glaring at him. "I truly am sorry, but I'd do it again if I wasn't so sure it would kill me too."

Sammy finally got up, but she was walking funny all the way to the bathroom. When she closed the door, he could grin again without upsetting her, and he did so. It made him feel like he'd just accomplished something profound to have his mate walking like she was sore just after having the most mind-blowing sex of his lifetime.

It was nearly noon when they were able to get up and get going. He didn't have any plans for today other than to get some furniture bought and get their house filled out. Just as they were getting ready to leave the B&B, the owner asked them if they would need an unlock code to get back in tonight. After telling her that they would, she gave them the four-digit code that would get them in after hours. He didn't know how long shopping was going to take, but he didn't need to be locked out of his bed tonight.

Glad they were both armed with lists, his for the outside and hers for everywhere else that they'd been adding to over the last few weeks, they were finally on their way. There was so much to purchase that they knew that they had to make several trips to the truck he brought just for this occasion. Then he remembered the gift that his mother had made for Sammy. He handed it to her then.

"This is a lovely bag. I'm going to use it today." He told her what it could do. "What do you mean it can hold a car and never be heavier than it is right now?"

"It's magical. It'll never stretch out, either she told me. So when we're shopping today, when we buy something, you can put it in that bag, and we'll be able to have it when we get to the house. And to get anything out of it, all you have to do is think about what you want while your hand is inside of it, and it'll fill your hand." She put his and her cell phone in the bag and lifted it up. "It's not much, but I'm betting by the end of the day, you're going to be glad for the bag. We can put linens and things in it to have when we get there. Also, before I forget, I've ordered a mattress and box spring for our bed. It has to be longer to accommodate my height and weight."

"I think it will be helpful for a lot of things that we do today." He nodded. "As for the mattress, I'll mark it off my list that it's done. I'm assuming that we're having everything larger than the opening of this bag delivered?"

"Yes, that's the plan. And if we have to pay extra to have it delivered tomorrow, that's fine with me too. Before I forget, my condo is ready for your dad to stay there. I've heard that he's being released in a couple of days." She said that's what she heard as well and asked about her mother. "She's still in jail. They can hold her until the circuit judge comes through in a few days."

"The longer she's in jail, the better I like it. I've been meaning to ask, how does this affect her parole? Will this be something that sends her back to prison?" He said he'd not thought of that, but would have someone look into it for them. "I was just wondering. When I was talking to Dad, he told me about their parole officer telling them that they had to have a residence as well as a job before he saw them the next time. I think I remember him telling me that his appointment with them is in less than a month. It wouldn't bother me at all if she were to end up in prison again. She's no one I want to have around messing with my life."

"I don't blame you at all." They were at the shopping center where there were several places they could purchase what they needed. Furniture wasn't anything that he enjoyed shopping for but spending the entire day with Sammy was something that he was looking forward to. "Okay, we're here. Which room did you want to start with? I'm assuming that we should start someplace and buy that one room at a time so that we're not all over the place buying things."

"I love that plan. Lets start with the living room. Since we can sleep on the mattress on the floor for our room, it'll be the last place we go to before the end of the day. That way we're not rushed into getting something that we don't really like but was there." He told her that was also a good plan. "I have them on occasion. All right, let's get started."

Most of their time was spent sitting on sofas and chairs. They had found one set that they both liked but the pattern on it was too much. And since they couldn't have it redone, they decided to skip it. They'd not like it any better in the house than they did here so there was no point in getting it. He thought that the pattern was more suited to a hotel lobby than a house but that was just him.

As they shopped, they also looked for little things that appealed to them. Like Sammy found a set of lamps that she really liked, and they bought them. Since they didn't find anything else at the store, she put them in the bag. They were both so amazed at the way they fit and were nicely packed away, they started finding other things that they could put into the bag to save them some trouble of having it delivered. He couldn't wait to see what they put in there next.

It was nearly two when they decided to stop for lunch. It was late in the afternoon which made it nice because nothing was very busy. They didn't linger long afterwards but got to work right away. He never thought he'd have this much fun shopping for stuff for their first and hopefully forever home.

By the end of the day, they not only had the living room finished up, but the dining room and two of the bedrooms as well. Their bedroom had been finished first, having found something that they both loved in the second store and the company didn't mind selling them an extra dresser for their room either. Of course, with enough money to make things happen, it was nice to be able to say that. He didn't know what they'd do if they'd not sold them an extra one but to keep on shopping, he supposed.

By the time the stores were closing up, they were more than thankful for the bag that his mom had given Sammy. Not only did they have towels in it, but all the linens that they needed as well. Even a few kitchen items were added in — such as a tea maker as well as a coffee machine for hot tea — they were thrilled when the bag never got any heavier than a few ounces. They'd even tried out the finding thing magic to see if it really did work. He didn't know why he questioned his mother's magic, but it was fun to see the joy on Sammy's face when she pulled out the lamp that she'd gotten for the living room.

Heading home, they got some dinner, and this time lingered a bit at the restaurant. They were both exhausted and yet still in a good mood for what they'd been doing all day. By the time they were at the B&B

again, it was late enough that they had to use their key code to get in. He was never so grateful for being in a small town than he was tonight. There was the trust that you never would get in a larger city.

Chapter 8

Sidney didn't mind going to his brother's house to help set up his home. He knew that Melbourne would do the same for him. It was just that he wanted to get his house in order so that he wouldn't have to be so late getting his home set up while his mate was just coming around. It took all his power not to tell his brother he should have planned better.

"What's the matter with you? You've been snipping at everyone all day." He told his brother Fowler that he'd not been doing that at all. "Yes you have. You made Amy pissed off. If not for me being there when you did it I think she might well have zapped you with some of her magic and that would have been the end of you."

"I'm just not in a great mood. Why did he wait so long in finding a house? They've been together for a month now. As it stands right now, we have to get everything off the truck tonight so that they're not sleeping at the bed and breakfast in town. Who plans things that way?" Fowler popped him in the back of the head once. "What was that for? If you don't agree with me that's fine but you don't have to try and take my head off."

"First of all, take it down a notch. I didn't hit you nearly as hard as I could have. Secondly, they've been dealing with their work schedule. Unlike the other wives, Sammy isn't going to give up her job just because she married into money. She likes what she does and is, from what I hear really good at running the restaurant. This was the only two days that she could get off in a row." Sidney said that they were still cutting it close. "Close to what? They have all the time in the world to get things set up. And if you didn't want to help then you should have stayed home."

"I don't mind working to help them out. But don't you think that this is a little rushed right now? I would have had my house filled out before I bought it." Fowler told him it didn't always work out that way. "I guess not. But I'm not one to leave things until the last minute. I plan to be living in my house when my mate comes along."

"Good for you. And what if she has a house of her own, like Amy did? Or one like Emma had? Then what would you do?" Sidney said that they'd end up selling one of them. "I think what Melbourne and Sammy are doing is great. One more thing that they can cross off their list. And from what I've heard, they had a list that they worked on together and purchased everything together as a couple. I like it that way."

They were asked to bring in the table and chairs for the dining room. It was a room that he decided that he liked more than the others that his brothers had. This one had a large table and twelve chairs that would fit around a round table that fit in the room well. There were also extra leaves to put into it so that they could enlarge it to fit as many as eighteen people, and it would not seem all that crowded. The round table would make for better conversations around the thing, he thought.

"How about you try to be nice instead of thinking that you'd do so much better? Look at the two of them, do they look like they're mad because they waited too long in buying a house. And according to Melbourne, they're helping out Mrs. Barnes who owns the B&B by stimulating the economy a bit. She told me that it surely did help her to have the place used when she would normally not have anyone staying." He said he'd not thought of that. "Well, they could have rented another condo that was bigger than where they're staying but they like being pampered a bit too. Mrs. Barnes runs a nice place and I'd hate for her to go out of business just because she doesn't have enough visitors coming around."

They not only got the table put together but also most of the chairs unboxed as well. When they were finished with the room, Sammy brought in the pretty sun catchers that she'd gotten to hang in the windows that were a perfect match to the place mats that she'd picked up too. Sidney thought that he'd like place mats over a table cloth more anyway.

The living room was about finished when they were done with the dining room. The three overstuffed couches looked great in the room, and he had to try out one of them to see if they were as comfy as they looked. Sure enough, they were more so, and he could see himself sitting here watching a game on the television while hanging out with his brothers.

"The television will be delivered in an hour. They said that they could even hang it for us if we wanted. We did spend a great deal in their store so I'm betting that isn't a service that they just offer to anyone." Melbourne thanked him for coming to help out. "I know you had a lot to do today but this is so much more fun than I thought it would be. We've even ordered food to pig out on while we break in the living room."

"I love your couches." He said that Sammy had picked them out and suggested that they get three of them. "She has great tastes. And the lamps go perfectly with them too. Like they were made for each other."

"They're from two different stores, believe it or not. The first store didn't have anything that we both liked — I love the fact that we were able to pick out our first houseful of furniture together. It made it seem more for us and not something that one of us would have picked out alone. I wouldn't have gotten this. It seemed to fluffy. But once I sat in them, I knew she was right."

"There's a lot to be said for doing something like this together, I guess." He told him that they'd picked out everything together, and it seemed more special for them. Sidney was beginning to see that his brother had done things up right, and he might well be doing the same thing. But he was going to get himself a bigger condo so that when he did find her, they'd have a place to stay before they got a house. "I heard that your father-in-law is staying at your condo. Is that all right with him?"

"Not only is he very happy that he isn't living in an abandoned house but he likes having more than four walls to look at too. He's going to stay there after he gets better too and his leg is healed. It makes it so much easier for his daughters to visit him as well." Sidney was helping Melbourne break down boxes when the food arrived.

They still had quite a bit to put in rooms but since the dining and living rooms were set up, they at least had a place to eat and to hang out. And he couldn't get over how much he loved the two rooms now that they were finished.

The food was a big hit and he was told that if they were still working at dinner time they'd be ordering out again. He could see that they were going to need to order out, as they not only had the kitchen items to unbox, but there were the library and bedrooms that needed to be put together, too. By the time he was finished with the first bedroom, just taking cardboard off the furniture, he was ready for his second round of food. And he'd also realized that the two of them had set up their home just the way he'd hope to do his own someday. But they'd done it together. He thought that was the point that Fowler was trying to make when he popped him in the head.

After the second bedroom was finished up, it didn't take nearly as long to unbox the things in the second bedroom as it did the first one, he was ready for a nap. There had been good food at the table when they'd all eaten and he needed to lie down. As soon as he got into the kitchen to help out there, Sammy came to find him.

"I was wondering if you could set up the computer as a surprise for Melbourne. It'll be nice to have them both set up but I know that he's missing some important investments that he'd be on top of but for the move." He told her that it would be his pleasure. "Thanks. I love that we both have our own offices so that we can work from home. When I was working from my home before moving here, I was using a board across two chairs to use for a desk. That's about all I had room for. But I can see myself spreading out in my office and not having to be at work so much. I love what I do but I do spend too much time there, I'm beginning to realize."

Sidney was glad to be doing something like this for his brother. And with all the help they were getting things squared away quickly. As soon as the television arrived, he noticed that his brothers were spending time in living room rather than in the rooms they were set to be working in. He had to laugh every time someone said that the furniture was almost too comfy to sit on, and they were hard-pressed not to take a nap.

Once the room was set up in his brothers office, he was jealous at the desk that had been delivered, he set to working on setting up the computer system. It was a new one too and again he was slightly envious of the fact that they'd gotten such a good computer when they moved in. After having it all set up, including the fax machine — something that he was going to keep in mind when he needed to fax something, he went into Sammy's office to set her up as well. Her desk was just as beautiful as his brothers had been but in a more feminine way. She had suncatchers in her office windows as well. He was just finishing up when someone mentioned food was going to be ordered and he'd not realized that he'd spend six hours just setting up the computers for his family. He was also starving again.

Instead of being pizzas and subs for them all there was massive amount of Chinese food delivered. Even though he didn't care for soup when he had his food, there were at least two gallons of hot sour as well as egg drop to enjoy. There were dozens of egg rolls to eat, and his favorite, fried dumplings. Since there were multiples of each thing, he didn't worry about them running out of food before everyone got their fill.

Everything was finished at about eight-thirty. Even the cardboard had been cut down into manageable strips that were going to be tossed in the recycling bins in town. Nothing was missing, he'd been told, but one of the couches had a broken leg that was going to be replaced by the store in the morning. The house for just being moved into looked like they'd been living in it for the past several years instead of less than twenty-four hours.

It was the finishing touches that made him realize that there were touches of both his brother and his mate in the house. There were little things that had been bought in mind of their first home together. In addition to the sun catchers in the dining room and her office, they'd managed to get comfy looking lap blankets for the back of couches as well as framed artwork that went with the rooms that they'd been bought for. There were decisions that the two of them made together that made the house look like a home and that was what they had intended.

By the time he was at his own home that night, he found himself looking around his place and being slightly ashamed of it. There was nothing personal in any of the rooms but for a picture of his parents together. He didn't have any lap blankets on the back of his one couch that had seen better days. The kitchen looked like a single person lived there with his one plate, fork and spoon. He didn't even have a good set of knives to use when he did get around to cooking, which wasn't all that often anymore. His bathroom was more drab than any of the other rooms. There wasn't any kind of a mess waiting for him but he really should have cleaned his sink off when he'd been in there this morning and now he had white toothpaste stains on the counter that looked out of place even for him. He wasn't a slob but if there wasn't someone coming in once a week to clean up after him, he didn't want to think about how badly the place would look. He thought of his brother hiring a cook and staff, and wanted the same thing as he did. But with his mate helping him level things out in a house that they picked out together.

Now all he had to do was meet her so that he could pick things out with her together. So they'd be as happy as his brothers were. It occurred to him that he was the last of them to find their mate, and he was sort of happy about that. But mostly he was afraid. He wasn't going to mess up like his brothers had, but be like Melbourne and go into it with an open mind and an equally open heart. His life's work was to make his mate happy and he was going to start that right now by being a better man than he'd been before. He wanted to be someone that she came to easily and happily. However he had a feeling that it was going to be nothing like his brothers were when they were mated and he was going to be left standing when she kicked his ass about something. Secretly he was happy about that too.

~*~

Belinda was to go before the judge in the morning to see when she could get out of the jail. She'd been as nice as she could be, much like she'd been in the prison when she was around the cops. They could make or break you when it came to having you in trouble with the judge and she wanted to be out to be free of all the curtailments that were driving her crazy by being locked up again.

She'd sworn when she got out of prison that she was never going to go back. She supposed that everyone said that. But she didn't like being in jail either. The very nerve of Allen pressing charges against her had her spitting mad. All she'd done was make a point about him giving her shit and knocked him down a few stairs. Now she couldn't find the slimy bastard.

When she'd stepped over him to leave the building, she had at least made sure he was breathing. She, of course, had to kick him a few times to get him out of her way, but that in no way made her a terrible person. She might well have fallen too if she'd tried to step around him he'd been laying at an awkward angle. People just didn't understand the relationship that they had between them. She thought that she was smart in only knocking him down the stairs and not really hurting him while he was down.

"Stupid people. Where do they get off putting me in jail like this?" She watched as the officer from this morning came down the hall. Usually, they made rounds about four times a day, more of them, she supposed, when she was sleeping. When he stopped in front of her cell, she was told that she had a visitor. It was her daughter, Sammy.

"Sammy? I thought that she was too busy with her new house." The officers here were very good at keeping her informed about the goings on with her family. None of them knew anything much about her as she didn't socialize much but they knew all there was to know about her soon to be husband. He was rich as they came and they'd just bought them a house.

A big one too she found out. But she couldn't get anything about her Allen. Where he was nor how he was doing. He'd better be just fine or she was going to give him something to whine about, damn it.

"Did you want to meet her back here or in the commons rooms? There are a few visitors in the commons room right now so you'd have more privacy back here." The thought of getting out of the cell was too overwhelming for her to think about a few visitors hearing her story with her daughter. "I'll take you back but you'll be chained up. That's what Sammy requested."

"Why?" He said that he didn't know but that was her request. "She'd better have a really good reason is all I can say. I haven't done anything wrong."

Or so they thought. She did what she was told to do to get out of the cell. They thought of her as a model prisoner and she was glad for that. Tomorrow when the judge finally came to town, she was going to make sure that he had no reason to throw the book at her. She'd heard from her parole officer that she might well end up in prison for another five years for breaking her parole when she'd been getting out. She didn't have a job nor did she had a good place to live. All things that she was going to make her daughter get for her.

After being chained to the table, she wanted to slap the smile right off her daughters face. Instead she sat there with what she hoped was her own smile so that she didn't look like she was worried about anything. The first thing out of her daughters mouth was to ask her why she'd pushed her father down the stairs.

"Is that what he thinks happened? I didn't push him. He was falling and I tried to reach out to grab him." She didn't say anything and Belinda had plenty to say yet. "He's just looking for sympathy and I won't have it. I've been in this jail for far too long over him thinking that I'd try to kill him."

"But you see I know that's what your plan was the entire time. You might not have heard this but I'm married to a shifter. And he's been able to read your mind about a lot of things you were doing when you got out of prison. I don't think that anyone is going to be happy to know that you've been stealing food from the local grocery store. Nor that you've been stealing mail out of peoples mail boxes. Then there is the fact that you nearly killed Dad by pushing him down the stairs five days ago to make him do what you wanted."

"Lies. You don't know what you're talking about." She had a feeling that she was being watched again and turned to look in the corner of the room where the cameras were. It wasn't the camera that bothered her but the feeling that she was being watched by something other than that. She looked at her daughter and forgot to hold onto her façade about being a victim of other people. "You know something about me being followed around too. I'm sure of it. That man, he has someone watching over me all the time. Doesn't he and don't lie to me, I'll kick your ass no matter how locked up I am. And you well know it too."

"There she is. The mother that I remember oh so well. How do you propose to do anything when you're locked down like the animal that you still are? I could get up and walk out of here and there would be nothing you can do about it." She told her that she wouldn't leave until she told her that she could. "We'll see. You never answered me about pushing Dad down the stairs. What would have happened had you killed him? You would have gone back to prison for sure."

"I told you. I was trying to grab him. And who cares anyway? I've not seen him around so he must be getting along all right. Where is he staying anyway?" She was told that he was in the hospital. "For what? A few bumps and bruises? He didn't fall down that many stairs that he has to have treatment for."

"You broke his leg. Not to mention a couple of badly bruised ribs from you kicking him while he was down." She told Sammy that he was in her way. "So you did just step over him, kicking him while he was down. Christ, mom. Is there any limit to what you'll do to hurt someone? Plus he has a concussion from hitting his head on the stairs when he fell. When you knocked him down the stairs."

"Oh, who cares how he got hurt anyway? He's more than likely going to expect me to take care of him when he's released. I'm not going to have it. I have things to do for myself." She told her what was going to be happening to dad when he was out of the hospital. "In that one bedroom place he was telling me about? There wouldn't have been any room for the two of us but he decided that that's where we were going to be staying. He's stupid if you ask me. Too stupid to know that he's being taken for a ride, I'm sure of it."

"He has a job too. Plus a place to live. Both requirements for your parole. You didn't do anything and have been arrested on top of that. What will that do for your staying out of prison again? Nothing, I can tell you that right now. As soon as you broke your parole rules, they can send you right back to prison without a trial. I hope that's what happens to you." She said she wanted a house and money. "No. I'm not going to provide you with either one and not a job either. I loved you being in prison and so does Justine. We're both happy about Dad; he seems to have gotten his shit together, unlike you, and is making something of himself."

"What kind of job does he have? Something beneath him no doubt. You should be thrilled to help us out now that we're both out of prison—a place where the two of you had us going in the first place." She said again that she liked her being in prison. "Well, I'm not going to go back because you have a burr up your ass about something. And why does your dad get your help and I'm stuck being in jail?"

"Because you tried to kill him. And I didn't give him the job. He works for my husband." She said she wasn't married. "Oh but I am. Melbourne and I tied the knot just this morning at the courthouse so that we can put each other on our accounts."

The two of them spoke for another hour without Belinda getting anything that she wanted done. Not only was Sammy not going to be helping her out but she'd been told that Justine wasn't going to be helping her either. How could they not want to help them when they'd not be around without her giving birth to the two of them?

Kids nowadays expect things to be handed to them on a silver platter or something. It was the damned phones, she believed. They were the ruination of the world as far as she was concerned. No one could do anything without a phone shoved up in their faces.

After being taken back to her cell, she could tell that someone had tossed it. They were forever doing that when she was in prison too. And since she had been caught with goods that she shouldn't have had, she'd been put in places that she didn't want to think about again. Solitary confinement wasn't a place she enjoyed nor did she want to do that again. While she didn't mind her own solitude, she couldn't stand herself for very long. She got on her own nerves. Tomorrow she'd be out and that would be the end of the shit going on behind bars.

Getting up at an ungodly hour to get cleaned up for her court appearance, she was sitting in the back of a cruiser waiting to be taken over when something touched her mind. Waving off the feeling, she was annoyed at first then she had a pause to wonder if it was Sammy's husband again reading her mind.

"No, I'm his mother." She asked what she wanted and was told to only think about what she wanted to say, and she'd get it. "That way, people won't think that you're crazier than you are right now."

"I'm not crazy at all. I'm not the smartest tool in the box but I can hold my own when I have to." The laughter that rang in her head had her looking around to see if anyone else could hear it. It sounded like bells ringing. Like the kind that had water flowing over them to make them sound. It was a sound that she thought that she could get used to. "Who are you and what do you want? I have to keep practicing for my trial today."

"You're going to fail. Because you want to know

why?" She said that she wasn't, and there was no way that she'd be able to. "Yes, you will because as of the second that someone asks you a question, you're not going to be able to lie. You're going to tell the truth no matter how much it pains you to do so."

"I don't lie." The laughter again, and she found herself smiling at the sound. "We'll see about how I can lie myself out of any situation. I've had plenty of practice."

"No doubt you have had plenty of practice. I would imagine that you've done it all your life. Well no more. You'll tell the truth starting with the next question asked of you. And not only will you only tell the truth, but you'll do it with a smile on your face." Then the laughter again that this time felt like a curse. "You'll enjoy it too, my dear pain in the ass. Hopefully this will get you all that you deserve when it comes to jail time."

"You can't do that to me. Everyone lies, I'm just better at it." Nothing. Not even a little bit of laughter that she was so fond of hearing. There was no way that she was going to be able to get by without lying, especially in a courtroom where she was going to be asked a lot of questions. She'd just have to figure out a way to make it so that she could lie without harming herself. She knew she could do it, too.

"Are you ready to go?" She had to bite her lip in

saying anything back to the officer who was taking her to the courthouse. It would figure that the very next question that she was asked was one about whether she was ready or not to face her crimes.

She was going to make it work if it was the last thing that she ever did. And she had a feeling that it was going to be the last thing that she did before heading back to prison. If she had to go, she was going to make sure that Allen went with her. He no more deserved to be free than she did to be in prison. The dirty bastard had told her that she was going to get her comeuppance once they were out. When all he wanted to do was to find himself a good job and a place to sleep at night, she'd wanted everything given to her so that she'd not have to fuss with anyone or anything again. Damn, but things never seemed to work out for her.

Before You Go...

HELP AN AUTHOR

write a review

THANK YOU!

Share your voice and help guide other readers to these wonderful books. Even if it's only a line or two, your reviews help readers discover the author's books so they can continue creating stories that you'll love. Log in to your favorite retailer and leave a review. Thank you.

AWARD WINNING, BESTSELLING AUTHOR

Kathi Barton, a winner of the Pinnacle Book Achievement Award and a best-selling author on Amazon and All Romance books, lives in Nashport, Ohio, with her husband, Paul. When not creating new worlds and romance, Kathi and her husband enjoy camping and going to auctions. She can also be seen at county fairs with her husband, an artist and potter.

Her muse, a cross between Jimmy Stewart and Hugh Jackman, brings her stories to life for her readers in a way that has them coming back time and again for more. Her favorite genre is paranormal romance, with a great deal of spice. You can visit Kathi online and drop her an email if you'd like. She loves hearing from her fans. aaronskiss@gmail.com.

Follow Kathi on her blog: http://kathisbartonauthor.blogspot.com/